ELECTRICITY
& OTHER DREAMS

ELECTRICITY
& OTHER DREAMS

SHORT STORIES BY

MICAH DEAN HICKS

new american press

Milwaukee, Wis. • Urbana, Ill.

n e w   a m e r i c a n   p r e s s

www.NewAmericanPress.com

Printed in the United States of America

ISBN 978-0-9849439-4-4

Cover design and interior art © Liz Green
Interior layout by David Bowen

For ordering information, please contact:

Ingram Book Group
One Ingram Blvd.
La Vergne, TN 37086
(800) 937-8000
orders@ingrambook.com

Grateful acknowledgment is made to the following publications, where previous versions of some of these stories appeared: "Dog Summer," *MAYDAY Magazine*, 2012; "The Alligators' Gods," *Indiana Review*, 2012; "Ladybaby's Chickens," *Art Faccia*, 2012; "When the Plumber Drank the Ghosts," *Bartleby-Snopes*, 2011; "Watermelon Seeds," *SmokeLong Quarterly*, 2011; "Cleaning the Fleaboy," *Bluestem Magazine*, 2011; "Gun Juggling," *Product*, 2011; "The Butcher's Chimes," *Menda City Review*, 2011; "Oldjohn's House," *A capella Zoo*, 2011; "In a City," *decomP magazinE*, 2011; "A Famine of Music," *PANK*, 2011; "Where the Electrician Went," *kill author*, 2010; "The Stickman's Cages," *Moon Milk Review*, 2010; "The Hairdresser, the Giant, and the King of Roses," *Sunsets and Silencers*, 2010; "Crawfish Noon," *Jersey Devil Press*, 2010; "How the Weaver's Wife Killed the Motorcycle Man," *Tryst*, 2010; "Dessa and the Can Hermit," *Prick of the Spindle*, 2010; "Railroad Burial," *The Smoking Poet*, 2010; "The Insulting of Warlord Reishi," *The Raging Face*, 2009.

CONTENTS

IV. THORNS

V. BONES

JASMINE

To ~~My Friends~~

You are the inventor,
turning all the world
to music.

Thanks so much for
your support.
— ~~illegible signature~~

SCALES

THE TIME OF THE WOLF

WHEN THE CONTRACTOR JACKSON walked into Abdul Karim's bazaar to buy a present for his son, he did not know that very soon he would die. That an eleven year old Arab girl would drive him out of town. That he would curl panting in a ditch as the shadows of the other contractors fell across him in the sun, their machine guns finding him in his hole. That his last sight would be the circling of birds, and his last thought would be to wish that he had listened to the shopkeeper's warning. All this in the deep desert, in no real country, a place they called Contractor Town. It happened this way.

A clutch of filthy birds squatted on the bazaar's roof, watching Jackson walk out of the white heat and into the narrow shop. He took off his sunglasses and blinked in the close, dim space. The floor was piled with boxes of things— books in sixteen languages, pieces of guns made by the Chinese and the Russians and the Americans, vinyl records stacked on CD players, headlight kits for cars no one had ever seen. The junk piles crawled up the carpet-covered walls of the shop where hung extension cords, bundles of military canteens, and Korean film posters. The objects reached the glass counters, precious stones flaring dimly beneath them. A small girl unboxed dishes on the floor and gave them prices with a sheet of stickers and a pen. The shopkeeper, Abdul Karim, smiled at Jackson from behind the counter. "Welcome," he said. "What might you be looking for?"

Jackson tugged at the front of his shirt, heavy with sweat, the black plastic buttons and coarse blue fabric sliding over his thumb. "I want to buy a gift for my son," Jackson said.

Abdul Karim showed Jackson what he had: crumbling books of poetry in Arabic, American Westerns dubbed in Japanese, designer watches that misspelled the designers' names. But Jackson shook his head at all of these treasures. "I want something that no one else has."

Abdul Karim led him over to the counter and brushed away the dust. "Each of these stones is pulled from the mountains and cut by hand," he said. "No two are alike."

Thinking his son would not like jewelry—though in truth, he did not know what his son liked—Jackson started to wave all this away, when he saw the round stone on the shopkeeper's finger. It was milky white, and light pooled in its center like the pupil of an eye. The stone was set in a ring of thin gold. Jackson felt that the stone watched him from the shopkeeper's hand.

"What is that?" Jackson pointed.

Abdul Karim straightened his fingers. "A jinn stone," he said. "A thing of magic. The story goes—"

"How much for it?" Jackson asked.

The little girl looked up at them from her place on the floor.

"Nibal, go play in the back," the shopkeeper said. He leaned toward the contractor over the counter. "The stone is cursed. Death follows it. A crime for me to sell it to you."

Jackson slowly looked around the shop, then back at the man. "You need my money," Jackson said. He said it and he believed it, the only thing he knew about this place.

Abdul Karim shook his head. "To have the ring is to use it, and to use it is to die. I only keep it so that no one else will suffer."

"I'll give you two thousand dollars," Jackson said. He pulled out his wallet and began putting the money on the counter.

"If I sell it to you, you must know the story." The shopkeeper's face had become very sad.

Jackson reached for a cigarette and leaned back on his heels to listen.

"Once, there were jinn in this country," Abdul Karim said, "and they were all powerful, but they feared the wolf. When the wolf came, the jinn would transform into stones to hide. But the wolf was clever, and he could smell a jinni anywhere. One day, the wolf found a magic stone and pissed all over it, trapping the unlucky jinni inside forever. While the stone lay in the desert, the phoenix heard the jinni crying to be free, and it slowly circled the spot, determined that whoever found the stone should die." The shopkeeper covered the white stone with his hand. "Anyone who holds the stone has the jinni's power. But anyone under the shadow of the phoenix will suffer the jinni's luck."

"Power?" Jackson asked.

Abdul Karim tried to think of what he could say that the contractor would understand. "It can stop bullets," he said.

Jackson held out his hand. The shopkeeper pulled off the ring, the band leaving an indention on his finger, and set the stone on the glass with a sharp click.

The contractor held the stone to the light and marveled. "The jinni's power."

"The jinni's luck," Abdul Karim said. "The phoenix will make sure you die."

Jackson left the money on the counter. He thanked the man and walked out of the shop, surprised at the ring's cool weight on his finger.

On maps, Contractor Town was called Oil Field Twelve. It centered around a cluster of aging oil pumps and refineries, following the pipelines snaking off into the desert. There were oil contractors who manned the wells and repaired the pipe, filled the barrels and sent them across the sea. Building contractors who salvaged scrap to make homes for themselves and others, who constructed towering, air-cooled palaces along streets without pavement or plumbing. Defense contractors who patrolled miles of pipe with their guns, toyed with attack helicopters and Humvees that the military had misplaced, who were hired to protect the town, but mostly got into fights with one another. And there were the people who'd been there first, those few who hadn't left, but instead stayed to live between tin and adobe walls and sell what they had for handfuls of foreign money.

Jackson went to the post office to mail the ring to his son, but found that the barred doors were already locked for the day. He went back to his home, a thin-walled cabin near dozens of others in a dirt lot, a chain-link fence around the compound. He cooked himself something on the stove, read over the old letters his family had sent, and finally went to bed. All evening, he had not taken the ring off. Outside his cabin, the top of the fence was covered in gray birds, tar dripping from their feathers and pooling on the ground.

Jackson lay awake for a few hours, but couldn't sleep. He got up and put on his work clothes, grabbed his keys, and went out. The contractors' housing compound was spotted with islands of light from windows and bonfires. Most were sleeping now, while others left or came back from shifts. On the wind, Jackson heard a stereo playing music, a woman singing in a language that was not his and not that of the town. He smelled spices he had never tasted from the open door of one of the cabins. A flag flew that he did not recognize. Contractors came from all over the world to work this desert.

Jackson walked all the way into town, the streets black and empty. He went to the refinery where he worked, turned on the lights, unlocked his toolbox, and began working on the machines. He worked until dawn.

Jackson sanded and cut metal, moved palettes of equipment, and made hundreds of welds, never stopping and never becoming tired. When the sun rose and he had finished all of his work, nothing left to do, he looked up and saw a company representative in a suit watching him from the plant across the street.

Jackson walked over and spoke with him. The man sent his entire crew of workers home and showed Jackson what needed to be done. Jackson worked all day, the sun moving in the sky and black birds streaming to the plant to watch him. He finished the work of ten in one day, and the company rep stacked money in his hands. On his finger, the ring burned.

When he had run out of things to do and finally went back home, Jackson saw the pile of faded envelopes from his family and rubbed the stone in his palm. He tried to think of another gift he could give his son, but nothing in Abdul Karim's bazaar was any better than junk. He wanted to give his son something unique. Only the stone would do.

Jackson walked towards the post office, old brick hotels throwing the skinny street into shade, making a wall of cooler air. A dog pissed onto a pile of concrete, and the runoff pooled in a hollow place in the middle of the road. When he turned a corner, he came across a cafe with a crowd of men smoking outside. They stopped talking and stood when they saw him, and Jackson knew that these were the contractors whose jobs he had taken.

He tried to walk away, but the men blocked his path. They all wore guns with the logo of one of the defense contractor firms on the holster, and they smelled of sweet tobacco.

"You owe us money," one of the men said.

Jackson shook his head. "I don't owe anyone anything. But I'll give you something."

He started to reach for his wallet, but the men misunderstood. Or if they understood, they didn't want to. When Jackson's hand reached across his belt, one of the men shot him.

Jackson saw the hammer of the gun drop four times. He heard four claps of thunder, and then he felt four thuds against his chest.

He looked down at his shirt. The fabric was not torn. There was no blood. The bullets were flattened discs lying beside his boot, smoking on the dirt. Jackson picked them up and marveled at their killing weight in his hand, balanced by the heaviness of the jinn stone in the other.

Everyone stood still for a long time. The men held their cold guns, blinked in the smoke and the sunlight, and wondered what was going to happen next.

Jackson walked up to the man who'd fired, grabbed him by the jaw, and pushed the four flattened bullets into the man's mouth one by one with his thumb. "What do you taste?" he asked.

The slugs rattled against the man's teeth as he spoke. "Metal. Gunpowder. Sand."

"No blood?"

The man shook his head. "No blood."

Jackson pinched hard on the man's cheeks, catching the wet bullets in his palm and putting them in his pocket. "You're going to give me all the money you have," Jackson told the men, "and then I'm going to report you."

They filled his hand, the bills stacking up on the back of his ring.

Now he knew that he could not give the jinn stone to his son or anyone else.

Jackson hurried to Abdul Karim's shop. A bird looked down at him from the roof. Its pale feathers were matted with oil, dripping from the tips of its wings and running down its breast. It regarded him for a moment, then flew away, leaving a splat of black tar behind it. Jackson remembered what the shopkeeper had said about the phoenix, but he had too much on his mind to worry about it.

When he walked inside, the shopkeeper rushed forward from behind his counter. The girl, Nibal, watched the two men, trying to be quiet so that her father wouldn't ask her to leave.

"You want to get rid of it?" the shopkeeper asked. "Before it kills you?"

Jackson handed him the four flattened bullets. "Nothing can kill me while I have the stone." Jackson paid the shopkeeper for four gold chains and had him attach a bullet to each one as a pendant.

Abdul Karim handed Jackson the chains and held his daughter against his side. "It will be your death," he said.

Jackson thanked him and left the shop. He mailed the chains and bullets that day, a gift for his two daughters, his son, and his wife.

Months later at Jackson's family's home, the package arrived. They opened the box with the four bullet necklaces. His two daughters, son, and wife put the bullets around their necks and wept. "He's dead," Jackson's wife said, "and these are the bullets that killed him." They pressed the metal against their skin and grieved.

With the jinn stone on his finger, Jackson became the greatest contractor who had ever lived. He didn't sleep and seemed to be everywhere at once. He edged out the defense contractors street by street. He told the company reps that no bullet could kill him, and showed them that it was true. He told them that they would be fools to pay anyone else for protection.

He returned to his job doing maintenance at the refinery and found that he could tell where a machine would break before it did, hearing flakes of rust pass each other in a joint and the suck of air slowly pushing through hairline fissures in a pipe. When Jackson stood near the pipeline, the oil flowed faster because he wanted it to.

On weekends, he moved pallets of sheetrock and cinder blocks by hand, slung up new hotels on the crowded streets in hours. One by one, the other contractors were told to find their own way home, their contracts lost by the companies they had worked for.

The other contractors met and decided that they would go to Jackson and ask him to stop. "Isn't he like us?" they said. "Doesn't he have a family and a home somewhere too?" After looking in all the refineries, they found Jackson sitting in an empty parking lot by himself. He was staring directly into the sun, drinking cartons of dirty engine oil and eating handfuls of sand. The contractors watched him do this for an hour, too afraid to speak to him. "We were wrong," they told one another. "He is nothing like us. He never was." They left to beg the company reps to give them work.

Jackson kept taking more and more jobs, piling up money in foreign bank accounts. Through all of this, flocks of oil-soaked birds fell on the town, all the street signs and roof edges dripping and black from them. They circled in the sky, following Jackson wherever he went.

The out-of-work contractors could not bring themselves to leave. They remembered filling trash bags with money in the back of the embassy. They remembered calling their homes in other countries and listening to their families name all the things they had bought. They remembered paying too much for tobacco, food, and foreign trinkets from the people of the town.

That night, they grabbed their guns, got in their Humvees, and rampaged through the shops and houses of Contractor Town. Contractors from Britain, the United States, Japan, Nepal, India, and elsewhere yelled in their varied tongues, burning and bombing everything they saw. They shot out windows and dragged people from their beds, making them reopen the cafes and serve them until dawn.

The people rioted the next day, and the contractors came out with their trucks and their guns to put the riots down. Again that night, the contractors burned and stole. Again, there were riots in the morning, and the graveyard on the edge of town began to stretch into the desert. It went on this way for weeks.

Across town, Jackson defended the company men's assets and repaired their buildings while sirens and the smell of smoke came to him from far away. He was too busy with work to understand what was going on.

Jackson stood outside Abdul Karim's bazaar. He'd run out of work for the day and had decided to ask the shopkeeper about the birds that followed him everywhere he went, but the shop was boarded up, the buildings on either side of it in ruin.

Through cracked and blackened windows, the other contractors watched Jackson force open the door and stumble into the dark bazaar. They saw birds descend and cover the roof of the building, and they loaded their guns. Something unlucky was about to happen here. They had known ill luck long enough that they could smell it.

As Jackson broke into the shop, Nibal had been walking in from the back, carrying a pot of urine. She and her father had no power and had been throwing their waste through a window for days, afraid to leave the shop.

"What's going on?" Jackson asked.

Nibal tried to speak, but she hated the man so much, she could form no words. She lunged forward and threw the pot of urine in his face.

Jackson fell to the floor and tried to wipe the stale piss from his nose, mouth, and eyes. It clung to him: a smell, a taste, a feeling. He screamed that he would kill the girl. He wiped his hands on his rough shirt, and the jinn stone slid wetly from his finger and rolled across the floor.

Nibal bent and picked it up, squeezing the stone so hard in her fist that it made her palm ache.

"You've ruined our lives," she told him. "Things are worse now than they've ever been."

There was the reek of urine. There was a burning in his eyes. "I will hurt you, girl," Jackson told her. "I will hurt you terribly."

"Am I afraid?" Nibal laughed at him. "Do you think you're the wolf?" She clutched the jinn stone and felt its warmth move up her arm. "Do you think even the jinn fear you?"

Jackson came toward her, raising his hand to take her by the throat. But Nibal struck him with her fist, the ring pressed between her palm and fingers, and Jackson's skin erupted into patches of gray fur. He fell forward onto all fours, transformed into the largest wolf she had ever seen.

Shrinking away from the stone that had changed him, Jackson slid on the rough floor and ran out of the shop. The contractors saw the great wolf flee the bazaar and run down the street, following the road that led away from town. They looked at one another and knew this was what they had been waiting for. They got into their Humvees and gave chase.

Inside the shop, Abdul Karim held his daughter and wept over her. She had used the stone. He knew that more ill luck would find them.

Out in the desert, the wolf hid behind cliffs or in hollows in the ground. But wherever he hid, the men always found him, following a chain of black birds that stretched through the sky, droplets of oil falling to sink into the dirt like a line of bruises. They shot him to pieces along the oil pipeline outside Contractor Town, running over his carcass. They brought the wolf back to town and skinned it, telling each other stories of how they'd killed the greatest contractor who had ever lived. They tanned the hide and kept it so that they would always remember. They signed up for new contracts with their companies, wrapping their stacks of money in the wolf skin and carrying it back to their cabins. They used the skin to cover the seats of their trucks and flew it like a flag from the rusted top of the refinery.

The birds always followed the pelt, swooping down to snatch at its edges with their beaks. The contractors chased them away, unwilling to give it up. Carrying the skin over his shoulder one day, a contractor saw a bird on a post watching him. Its feathers were gray and its eyes were blue, but its body was caked in tar and black leaked off it onto the post. It stank like the refinery. The contractor was sick of the birds that had invaded the town. He took the cigarette out of his mouth and jabbed the bird. It was too heavy with oil to get away in time.

The bird's feathers lifted in the heat as fire swept over its body without consuming it. All over town, each of the oil-soaked birds burst into flame wherever they were and rose into the sky. Their cries became loud and shrill until one great keening sound moved over Contractor Town.

Looking out their windows, the natives of the town, the contractors, and the managers all saw the sky turn red and the great burning shape lift itself. They shut their windows and cowered on the floor. They did not need Abdul Karim's story to know to be afraid.

The pelt was left lying in the middle of the dirt street. The flaming birds gathered in the sky over it, their fiery bodies licking in and out of one another like one thing, and all at once they came swooping down, a flood of fire, beaks, and rolling eyes. They picked up the pelt in their claws and carried it away.

The birds left Contractor Town. They went far beyond the desert, passing above gray cities. They came to the blue edge of the ocean and flew across it. They burned in day and night, in rain and sun. At last, they reached a land of square green yards, traffic lights, and rows of white houses. A place where sprinklers cast water through the air and dogs ran along chain-link fences.

From inside their house, Jackson's grieving family saw something through the kitchen windows. Fire fell from the air and spilled across their yard. It screamed in the voices of birds, lifted itself from the grass, and was gone. It had left their lawn and shrubs withered from the heat, a crescent-shaped smear of tar across the yard, and a gray wolf skin lying at their door.

Jackson's son went outside and brought back the pelt. He wrapped it around his shoulders and held it against his skin. "Father sent it," he said, crying.

They told him that his father had died months ago.

"No." The boy held the skin even tighter. "This proves Father is alive," he said. "He sent the wolf skin because it saved him. It can stop bullets."

THE ALLIGATORS' GODS

THEY MET ON A FRIDAY after work, the three men in their fifties. Mitch, the youngest, brought a heavy drum of yellow rope. James, the middle one, brought his old truck. Sawyer, the oldest, brought the same cheap twenty-four pack of supermarket beer he always did.

"We need an ice chest," Mitch said, getting into the truck.

Sawyer nodded. "Meant to bring one."

"You two always say that," said James.

They drained their cans, crushed them, and tossed them into the floorboard where the shifting mass clattered and rolled under their feet with every bump, the old beer smell mixing in the air with wide bands of pale cigarette smoke. This truck was more their place than anywhere else in the world.

They drove down into the swamp, the speakers in the doors shuddering with the static of distant radio stations, their windows rolled down. Mitch tried to change it to an NPR broadcast on the space station, but the other two called him a shit-ass and changed it back. While James drove, Sawyer and Mitch turned their spotlights out into the swamp. Alligator eyes glittered from the muddy banks and drifted in the moss-clotted waters.

The men parked their truck and got out, popping their backs and knuckles, nervous energy buzzing in their bones. Laughing and singing along with the music, they rushed the banks with their spotlights and dropped nooses around alligator snouts. They wound their ropes around trees while the animals thrashed, letting them buck and pant through their teeth, slitted eyes wide, and dragged them back to the truck once they'd worn themselves out.

They had little alligators, dog-sized alligators, and big alligators. They tied them down across the hood of the truck, tied a few across the top. They draped rope over the sides and artfully knotted alligators into slings along the back fenders. Little ones were strung up behind the tires like mud-flaps, and one was even tied across the dash, its tail hanging out the window.

Mitch rested his elbow on an alligator head while Sawyer tied it down. "You know," he said, "it seems to me that this god is most likely some kind of a painter or sculptor or some such thing. An artist god."

James heard him and came around from the front of the truck, walking his gator like a dog. "And how did you come up with something like that?"

"Well, you think now. An artist makes something, spends a lot of time on it. It is not without beauty, but we often don't have the clear reckoning of what it's for, and truth is that it ain't much good for anything. And then after the artist finishes, he moves right along and makes something else, don't ever come back to or think nothing of his old paintings no more."

Sawyer belched. "I like it all right. It does explain the human condition of feeling alone, and the reason why so many prayers go unanswered."

James shook his head and hoisted his alligator onto the hood. "You are some odd fuckers, the both of you. We'll come up with something better than that."

After loading the truck with alligators, claws scrabbling on the old metal and throats chirping fearfully, the men got back in the truck and plowed down muddy back roads, slamming through puddles and pits, thick black mud splashing over the truck so high that they had to pull the alligator tail inside and roll up their windows. The one dry gator rubbed his tail along their chests, listening to the sounds of his brothers outside.

Alligator tails swished back and forth, smearing the mud on the windshield, the truck's body shaking from their movement. "I believe they like it," Sawyer said.

"Oh, gators likes mud," said Mitch. "It's a fact of science."

James held out his hand for another beer. "I'd feel right terrible if they didn't."

They buried the truck up to the doors in mud. James stood in front of the hood and dug around for his winch, shoving alligator legs out of the way, and tying the cable around an oak tree to pull them out with a great sucking sound, the gators opening their mouths to the air. Then, they pulled back onto the main road, the wind hardening the shell of mud on the alligators' backs and making them sleep in their dirt cocoons.

Town was empty this late at night, but they found an automated car wash and put in a few dollars. "All they got's cherry wax. I don't even like cherries," James said.

Sawyer shook his head. "Never understood how a man can not like a cherry. In any case, we muddied them, so we got to clean them."

James pulled into the wash and the machines came alive, brushes and foaming jets falling onto the truck. The alligators woke up and made shrill throat-sounds, their claws clicking against the truck like a swarm of insects.

"Now, the problem," James began, "with this artist theory is that it don't take into account the whole scope and breadth of human religions, see? I think the god is more of an au-to-bo-dy-re-stor-er. Kind of man who takes your old beat-up, shit-heap of a car and makes it into something that can win a car show, sells it to some rich fuck who don't even drive the thing, and it rots in a garage somewhere for the rest of its life, or until his rich shit-for-brains son wrecks it trying to get out the driveway."

"How exactly does that account for all that breadth and scope you mentioned?" Mitch asked him.

"Well, it's a simple thing, ain't it? The planet is a car. We done had religion after religion fix it up and drive it for a while, then we get another, and so on. Currently, we're all fixed up, but we're sitting in a showroom somewhere, waiting to be wrecked."

"There's all kinds of religions, though," Sawyer said.

"Yeah, but only one of them is really with it at a time. Right now, it's your protestants. Your others done had their chances."

Mitch shook his head. "That sounds mighty eth-no-centric to me, you just leaving out all India and the Middle East like that."

"You just give me some time," said Sawyer. "I can top both of you."

After pulling out of the car wash, they saw that the alligators had gone pale, all the green and roughness scrubbed off of them. Their skins were so tender from the blasts of mud and pressure-washing that they had gone pink and soft, moaning from the ropes cutting into their skin.

"Hell," James said. "We can't take them back to the river, not puny as this."

"And what do you reckon we do with a truck-load of wimpy gators then?" Sawyer asked. "We can't just leave them in the parking lot at the Walmart."

"We done left stranger things out there," said Mitch.

The three watched the town lights play across the alligators' slick backs, when they noticed that something strange was happening. The red and yellow lights of liquor stores, fast food restaurants, and pawn shops fell across the alligators and saturated their skins, soaking into them. They curled up in their ropes, their noses blunted. They were starting to become men.

"Do you see what the light is doing?" Sawyer asked. "Go drive around the titty bar."

James turned off the main road and went out to the strip club, a haze of pink and green lights on the gravel parking lot. He looped the building until the alligators' limbs had lengthened into legs and arms. They swore and shivered on the sides of the truck.

"If lights is what makes you a person," James said, "then what were we in the dark of the womb?"

"You was a tadpole to begin with," Mitch told him. "All your modern sciences agree on this point."

Sawyer looked at the alligator on the dash: green, dry, and completely alone now. "I feel bad for this one." His friends nodded.

They drove back to Sawyer's house. He went inside and came out with several old pairs of jeans, plaid shirts, trucker hats, and a pile of old tennis shoes.

"You ever thrown a goddamned thing away?" James asked him.

Sawyer did not respond, but stroked the alligators' new faces. "It's a hell, being born," he told them.

They cut the alligators loose, except for the one still tied to the dash, and watched them wrap their arms around themselves and huddle together in the yellow floodlights of the house. The three men tossed the clothes to them, and the alligator-men put them on.

"I believe I have it," Sawyer said. "When you look at the ratio of water to land on this planet, coupled with the seasonal pollen, it stands to reason that god is a distiller and this planet is a barrel of liquor." His friends did not look convinced, so he continued, the alligators walking unsteadily on two legs around the truck. "We're fermenting, see? Everything's real lively right now, but one day we little yeasties will be done, everything in the barrel will die, and it will just be smooth whiskey."

"I ain't never much thought of myself as a yeast," James said.

"Well I like it," said Mitch. "I think it explains a lot."

One of the alligator men adjusted his hat, and holding up his pants with one clawed hand, he approached the men.

"Is god really a distiller?" it asked.

"There is some disagreement on what the god is," James said. "And on what all this is for. We never really get nowhere with it."

Another alligator came forward. "Why did you do all that to us?" he asked.

Mitch shrugged. "We was drunk pretty good. We just do things sometimes."

"Maybe that's what god is," the alligator said. "He just got drunk and whipped all this up one night. He don't even know why."

Sawyer looked at the others. "Well shit. That ain't bad, is it?"

"From the mouths of gators," James said.

"Or," said another alligator, "maybe god is a great big alligator, and he made this muddy wet place to crawl down inside to get away from the sun."

Mitch shook his head. "Most people's conception of the almighty is in form like unto themselves. It's hardly surprising a gator would conceive of a gator-god. I'm not sold on it, though."

"Now who's being eth-no-centric?" James asked. "I'd like a gator god, tell you the truth."

"I like it," said Sawyer.

"Well, it feels less depressing somehow than all that drunk god business. But if god's a gator, what would that make us?"

"We are the lice in his scales," one of the gators said, throwing his arms wide. The other one nodded, passing around cans of beer from the truck. Pretty soon, the gators drank them out. James tied the snout of the dash gator shut, put it on a thick leash of rope, and handed him over to his brothers. The three friends said goodbye, then, and left the alligator-men on the lawn to find their own way in the world.

The alligators went back into the sun the next day, but their bodies stayed small and pink. They kept their clothes and found factory work. They roomed together in a run-down apartment complex not far from the swamp, slipping out at night to drink beer on the bank and to try and woo old alligator lovers. They thought about their future. Should they buy better health insurance? Start a savings account? Try to go to college? Everything was new and complicated, the sounds of their old life buzzing just outside the windows.

The next weekend, the three friends met at a gas station after work. Mitch rolled a drum of yellow rope out of his car and put it into the back of James's old truck. Sawyer walked out of the store with a twenty-four pack of beer under his arm. They leaned against the truck and took off their hats, rubbing their heads. The door opened, and one of the alligator-men walked out of the gas station carrying a Styrofoam cooler and a bag of ice.

The three friends looked at one another.

"Hey, man," James said. "You want to come driving with us?"

The alligator hitched up his pants. "That sounds all right, I guess."

"What's your name?" Mitch asked him.

"I go by Rafael."

Sawyer nodded. "Something amphibious about that name. I always did think so."

"How's that alligator doing?" Mitch asked. "The one that didn't change."

"He's doing all right," Rafael said. "We got to hide him from the landlord. But he stays in the bathtub mostly."

The four of them packed into the truck and pulled out onto the road, a hot breeze rippling through the cab, an icy can in each of their hands.

"I do like having a cooler," Sawyer said.

"Rafael, you gators got anything new to say about god?" James asked.

Rafael took a drink and swallowed, his alligator throat jumping. "We been cooking up some things. You want to hear about it?"

The men nodded that they did and passed around a crushed pack of cigarettes. Rafael looked out the window toward the swamp, his tiny ears filling with the sounds of dragonflies and bullfrogs. He started telling them about the alligators' gods.

CRAWFISH NOON

THREE YEARS PAST, Seven-leg and his troop of hard-backed killers were knocking over settler wagons in the pines of east Texas. They had been in camp one morning, chewing rotten horse hides and Seven-leg dealing a round of cards, while they waited for one-antennaed Willy Moseley to get back with news about a job. Willy never showed, but the state militia side-crept on them and let loose loose with rifles. The bandits drew iron, swung their segmented bodies around, and shoved themselves underneath logs and rock piles. That day, the dirt flushed with blue blood, scraps of shell and leg segments strewn like cards. They lost a lot of good crawlers in those trees before they could get away. But now Seven-leg had heard about Willy turning sheriff in a border town, and his claw itched to squeeze down on his Colt cannon and make meat of the mud-eater who had betrayed him.

A gambler, Seven-leg was bringing six leadslingers for the job, all crawlers who'd been with him in the pines years ago, totaling seven: himself, Greg Potts, Tom Boiled, Janey Flicker, Nate Sayers, Coy James, and Dean Mitchell. Some of those crawlers would go on to become legends of their own, and some would go back to the mud.

It was two weeks swimming backwards downriver, their tails thumping through the mud-waters and reed-beds making good time. Nobody carried much more than their gun, the duster on their carapace, and pounds of shells.

Wouldn't need anything else. They came to a little town on the riverbank, nothing but a few dozen badly stacked mud chimneys, and Seven-leg told them to have themselves a good time. There'd be desert tomorrow.

Nate, Coy, and Dean found a dark saloon with just enough light for their cards, and stayed at that most of the night. Janey Flicker took some old shells to a gunsmith and had him fill them with powder and put new lead caps on them. She wasn't one to run out of bullets. Old Greg Potts wandered the town for a few hours, his eyes slowly clouding up like dishwater. He found Tom Boiled carrying around a tin bucket, putting out cook-fires, and shook his head. Ever since Tom had tumbled into a hot spring, something had been off with the crusty son of a bitch. Greg took the bucket away from him. He said he didn't know if he was up to crossing the desert, old as he was and all. Tom's mouth fizzed a little. He told Greg that if he backed out now, Seven-leg would get off Janey just long enough to put a bullet in him. Then, Tom said, he'd eat every piece of Greg himself. Greg called him a flat-tailed crazy piece of shit and crawled back to the saloon, but he was afraid Tom might be right. The next morning, Potts's eyes were solid gray with sick and he could barely see. Seven-leg asked him if he was going to be able to make it, and Tom grinned his burned grin. Greg spat and said that he could.

Out of the river, it was three days crawl across the heat wastes, nothing but sun and sun, and old Greg Potts died. That night, with a yellow moon heavy to fall in the sky, Seven-leg said some words over his shell. They sectioned up Potts, held the meat in their claws, and seared him red over the fire. That night, Nate, Coy, and Dean played cards while Janey Flicker fucked Seven-leg under the open sky, her five pairs of spinnerets drumming on his shell and his claw tugging her antennae. Off away from the others, Tom Boiled stuffed his mouth with Potts's legs and sang every song he could remember. That night, Seven-leg whispered to Janey that they were six now and had lost their luck, but as long as she was with him, he thought he could do anything.

Morning came, and Tom Boiled was up firing rounds into the face of the sun, bright red splotches shining on his back and head. Coy spat and said they ought to kill him for it, and Janey said she was sympathetic to that. The shots echoed back and forth to the horizon. The town was an hour out, nothing but flatland, and sure Willy would know they were coming now. Seven-leg told Boiled to get his shit straight, and Tom calmed down. Seven-leg pulled his hood over his rostrum, antennules checking the wind, and told them to get stepping. It would be a hot noon.

The town was a tiny hump on the desert, no more than a hundred crustaceans and larvae taken together. Adobe burrows ringed a few good-sized rocks. There was a clump of wood buildings warped and sun-bleached and all sharing walls with one another. Seven-leg's mouthparts rubbed together and he thought how generous it was of the militia to hide Willy all the way out here. He stuck a seven of clubs in his hat-band for luck.

They circled around to the south, knowing Willy had heard the shots. Tom Boiled was steady babbling, revolver clutched in each claw, not making any sense. Nate was fed up with it, but didn't see anything they could do about it now, so he kept quiet. Nate, Coy, and Dean threw their serapes back off their claws and drew iron. The troop crawled up the street in a line.

Seven-leg could see Willy's burrows on the north end of town, right where he thought they'd be. Bead-like eyes followed them from street windows, but no one moved until a larva ran out in front of Tom Boiled—scrawny thing, not much past a nauplius—and Tom skewered it with one sharp foreleg, shoved it in his mouth, and ate that little bastard with his parents watching from their door. Shit got bad then.

The town crustaceans screamed and drummed their claws on the walls. Willy spun around in his burrow, silver star gleaming on his carapace. He saw Seven-leg and his group down the street, and he and his deputies came boiling out, guns high and hammers dropping. Ducking into houses, Seven-leg and his troop were some cold-water killers, and raked the streets with lead from one end to the other. Seven-leg found himself alone in a doorway, a family balled up together on the floor behind him, and deputies sending gunfire his way. He shot back, wondering where Janey was, but he knew he couldn't worry about that now. He got hit, a bullet cutting straight through his tail and shattering the chitinous plate above it. It left blue stars of blood every time his tail slapped the ground, but that wasn't going to stop a crawler like him. He cleaned out everyone on the street, their antennae lying limp in the dirt, and went to find Willy.

There was an awful sound back around a cluster of cabins, and Dean wondered what in the hell Tom was doing over there. He saw Janey start scuttling that way. Willy's men were filing past the general store to stop her, but Nate, Coy, and Dean shot the bastards from an alley, their heads settling like helmets in the dust.

Seven-leg followed the shine of a silver star creeping in and out of water troughs and barrels, squeezing off bullet after bullet, stripping the tops of railings and hearing the sound of shells sink into Willy's soft body. He finally caught up with him trying to climb back into his burrow on the north side of town. Willy was walking in circles, his eyes gummed up with blood and dirt, antennaeless now, his sides dotted with shots. Seven-leg was glad he'd found him before he'd been able to drag himself into a hole and die. Willy flailed his claws, and Seven-leg crawled right up on his back and clamped two pincers behind his head. He asked if Willy remembered the night Seven-leg dug him out of jail and gave him his life back. Willy vomited a necklace of blue froth, slurred that he hadn't had anything to do with the ambush, and asked what the hell this was about. Seven-leg clamped down, Willy's heavy head dropping into a water trough. It floated there. Seven-leg spat on him and went to find the others.

Everything had quieted down. He found Nate, Coy, and Dean stacking bodies in front of the saloon. They were passing a bottle of whiskey back and forth, but Dean dropped it when they heard more gunfire at the cabins. Seven-leg raised the Colt in his right claw and went straight down the street while the others covered him. He came around the side of a building and saw Tom Boiled's bright-splotched head cracking apart under gunfire, some crawler standing over him and squeezing off shots into his body. Seven-leg didn't hesitate. He put a bullet down the center of her tail, blistering its way across nerve-bundles and burning out her head. Janey Flicker dropped her gun and fell down across Tom. Seven-leg howled and tore the dirt when he saw what he had done.

They found where Tom had smashed in the door of a nursery and stuffed himself bloated with little ones, then carved up those he couldn't eat. One girl's gray jelly skin was freckled with white spots where he'd tried to burn her.

Janey Flicker lay upside down in the dirt, her head a mess from gunfire, her spinnerets white and delicate and shining in the sun. Seven-leg lay down across her. He still had the seven of clubs in his hat. Nate, Coy, and Dean each took out their deck of cards, pulled the sevens from the stack, and dropped them beside the couple in the dirt. Seven-leg took her body in his claws and dragged it away, moving backwards down the street. They let him go, hoping he'd take his luck with him.

That night, Nate, Coy, and Dean played cards and ate the dead in front of the saloon. Seven-leg watched the dark from the mouth of his burrow, Janey cold underneath him. He tore off chill pieces of her and ate them, each one a reminder of how much he'd loved her. When Nate, Coy, and Dean came to get him in the morning, he was gone, seven needle-like tracks going off into the deep desert. They never met up with him again after that, heard later that he had gone further south and had run-ins with the army. They went back to Texas for a while, eventually farther west. They sowed stories wherever they went, shadows that grew larger with every saloon they passed. Though they never saw him again, every once in a while Seven-leg's stories would meet theirs around a campfire, behind a hand of cards, under a yellow moon.

THE SISTER'S WAR

A BIG HOUSE STOOD at the top of the highest hill. In it lived the father, his ten sons, and his ten daughters. The world was empty then, and the father ruled it. This was at the start of things.

All the animals—from meadow, river, and cloud—came to the father in his great house, and he commanded them as their king. Birds overlapped their wings in the sky, shading wolves who sweat beside goats and tilled the land around the house, planting pear orchards and fields of corn. Inside, the ten brothers and ten sisters prepared the food, added onto the house, and scrubbed the floors. The father was pleased.

Everything changed when the father died.

The brothers and sisters found him under a tree, a crowd of rabbits cocking their heads and marveling at his still body. His eyes were closed, his hands in his pockets. The siblings sent the animals away and marveled themselves. They hadn't known something like this could happen.

There being no burials in those days, the siblings placed the father in his bed and turned out his light. Telling the sisters to go back to their chores, the brothers gathered on the lawn to choose a new father from among them. They argued all afternoon, their hands in their pockets. But the brothers could not choose. Weren't they all old enough? Weren't they all wise enough, strong enough, tall enough?

Inside the house, the sisters crept into their father's bedroom and started going through his things. Before this day, they'd never been in his room before. They dug through the two deep closets, both chests, the two wardrobes. Their father had two of everything. They found dresses that were not theirs. Notes with handwriting that didn't match anyone they knew. Their dead father lay in his bed, his pale mouth telling them nothing.

The sisters realized that once, before any of them could remember, there must have been a mother. Outside, the shadows of the brothers still argued on the grass and the shapes of birds drifted by the window. The sisters passed the secret from ear to ear and joined hands. "We sisters will keep this for ourselves," they said.

On the lawn, the brothers argued until the moon rose and their voices gave out. Around them, the grass was thick with lizards and mice, listening and waiting for something to be decided.

In the light of the rising sun, the brothers saw that they all had the same dark silhouette. They could not tell themselves apart. When they spoke, it seemed one voice, and when they moved, it seemed one being. Looking around, they understood what to do. They linked their arms together and pronounced to all the land: "We brothers will rule."

From their feet, small beasts rushed away into every corner of the world, announcing what had happened.

Inside, the ten sisters had been clustered around the windows, and they had heard their brothers. They thought of how hard it had been under their father—scouring the floors of the great house, harvesting and canning the crops, spinning thread into fabric until their fingers ached.

"We will be divided between our brothers," they said. "Each of us will do the work of ten."

Knowing that they had to save themselves, the sisters took their pillow cases and filled them with everything that they could carry: bread, knives, clothes, grapes, hammers, egg-timers, picture frames, jam jars, and hairbrushes.

As the brothers came into the house through the front door, the sisters left through the back.

They walked into the tall grass of a wilderness without end. As they traveled, they drew farther and farther apart, until each of them was alone. They lived this way for years. The wild lands were a hard place, and the seasons moved quickly from blazing heat to freezing cold. They built their small houses in the middle of forests, in the mouths of caves, and beneath hills. They never saw one another again. Some died. None were mourned. But even apart, they kept their secret from the brothers.

The brothers soon left the house of their dead father and let it fall into disrepair. They divided up the land and ruled over every animal, from the deer steaming in the thickets to the eel nosing among cold stones in the river. Each of them commanded a new house to be built for himself, bigger and grander than where they had once lived together. They worked the animals hard, sending them to sweat in factories or to bruise their paws in black mines. Looking at their riches, the brothers congratulated themselves on being stronger kings than their father had been.

One day, a fox walked away from the assembly line during its shift. He outran the wolf foreman who chased him, ignored the jeers from the horses and cattle working the fields, and disappeared into the green rushes and lake country where he had been born.

After days of looking back at his prints in the mud and wondering if he would be found, the fox came to a squat house beside a lake. Curious, he knocked on the door. It was answered by a small woman in a dirty dress.

She brought him inside. "What is it you want, fox?" she asked.

The fox recognized her as one of the sisters who had run away so long ago.

"Ten brothers are too many," the fox said. "Isn't there anything you can do to help us?"

The woman looked around the tiny house, wondering what had become of her sisters. She remembered their small hands in hers, their voices in her ear, their hair in her face, and suddenly she hated her brothers very much.

"I will help you," the sister said. "But I will need time to think."

While the fox curled up and slept in front of her fire, the sister went through every cupboard, trying to find the pillow case she'd brought with her from her father's house years and years ago.

When the fox woke up the next morning, she set a pair of old boots in front of him.

The fox sniffed the boots and said that he didn't understand.

"Take one boot," the sister said, "and bring it to any brother you like. Tell him that it was his father's, and you bring it as a gift. But tell him that one of his brothers stole the other from you while you were on the road, and that's why you only have one."

"What do I do with the second boot?" the fox asked.

"Go to a different brother and tell him the same."

The fox snorted. "Why should the brothers care about old boots? Every one of them has a shoe factory of his own."

"They will care," the sister said. "They care about nothing else."

The fox did as the sister had told him. He took the first boot to a brother who lived in a brick tower above a waterfall, alligators with muddy backs carrying visitors to his door. "I was bringing you your father's boots," the fox told him. "But on my way, one of your brothers tried to steal them from me, and now I have only one."

The brother sat on his throne and turned the boot over in his hands. "So, so. One of my brothers thinks that he's the father," the brother said. "I'll take care of him."

The fox went to a different brother who lived in a cathedral on the plains, his house ringing with copper bells that families of deaf moles polished day and night. The fox told this brother the same story. "So, so. One of my brothers thinks that he's the father," the brother said. "I'll take care of him."

The fox did not have to wait long to see the brothers' rule fall apart. Each of the men with a boot went to their brothers and interrogated them, asking who had stolen the boot from the fox and why. Every brother denied that they had taken it, and they all became angry. "Why did you take it?" said some. "Why do you want it?" said others. Every brother who saw the boot wanted the pair for his own feet. He imagined that the shoes would fit him best of all.

War broke out between them. The brothers turned their canning factories and steel mills to making bombs and tanks. They outfitted battalions of thin-nosed rodents with cheap rifles, put wide-eyed hares in the seats of biplanes, gave batteries of artillery to their mules. The animals fumbled the bayonets in their hooves, crashed bombers, set fire to sandbags, ate up their rations, and made a pitiful war on each other.

In a few years, it came to an end. The wind carried pollen mixed with ash over the land. Factories had been shelled and farms had been burned. The brothers' fine houses were torn down. When the hulks of machines had rusted down to dust, the bones of animals rose from beneath them with the skeletons of the ten brothers in their mouths.

The fox returned to the lake country and found the home of the woman who had given him the lie. He had lost a leg in the war and had to pick his way slowly over the slick stones near the house. He knocked, and when the door opened, the fox was greeted by a house full of children.

The small siblings chased each other around the cottage, fighting and yelling and pulling hair, brothers mingling with sisters. The fox was amazed.

"Where did all of these children come from?" he asked the woman.

"Once, there was a mother," she said. "And I can do as much as she."

The fox lay his head on the floor and closed his eyes. "None of that matters," he told her. "Your lie hurt. It ruined the land, and it killed the brothers. How could you do such a thing?"

The children became quiet. They stared at the woman to see what she would say.

"It was not my lie if it was in your mouth," she told him.

The fox thought about this, amazed that he could have lied, and that his lie could have done so much.

"Who will rule now?" the fox asked.

"Someday, these brothers and sisters will be old enough to rule together," the woman said. "But not for a long time. Until then, there can be healing and rest."

The fox thanked her and went to the forest. The whole way, he licked his muzzle with his lying tongue. He thought of the power his mouth had and how the land would be without a king for many years.

He came to the middle of the forest and told the sparrows to fly away and bring the animals to him. When all the animals were gathered, the fox stood on a rock above them all. He spoke.

"My words killed the brothers," the fox said. "And my words burned down their factories and their farms, and my words stopped the machines that are dead on the plain. Now I will rule."

And all around the fox, the animals bowed and moved to serve him. They built him a fabulous home in the middle of the wood, filling it with ripe beetles, bottles full of caterpillars, and rolls of moss. They brought him milk and combed his fur. They carried him down to the river and back three times a day.

The fox smiled at his servants, knowing that this could not last forever. Across the plains, there were children growing taller every day, wandering farther and farther from their small house, taking more and more of the world as their own. One day the animals would find them, and the fox would have to explain.

But he was not worried. He would have new lies ready by then.

LADYBABY'S CHICKENS

LADYBABY IS AN OLD, OLD WOMAN these days. Ladybaby decide she gonna buy some chickens. Put em in her grown daughter's old playhouse in the backyard. Ladybaby is outside in that August sun, tacking chicken wire over the windows with a tiny hammer. That's how serious she is.

Her neighbor, Bubblegum, is an old man. He's a history teacher. He ride a bicycle places not because he don't have a car, but because he always talking about the planet. He always talking about a lot of things. Ladybaby sick of listening.

"Ladybaby, what you doin over there?" he ask.

"I'm gonna get me some chickens," Ladybaby say. "They gonna be so pretty. So, so pretty."

Bubblegum shakes his old head. "No, Ladybaby, you don't want no chickens. Chickens is hard to take care of. Chickens can be mean. You got that playhouse wired up so good, you need to get you a ferret."

"I don't like ferrets," Ladybaby say, but she ain't never seen one.

Bubblegum grins. "Ladybaby, you so pretty. But have you ever seen a ferret? Ain't nobody don't like a good, long ferret. Plus, they good for the environment. Put out less carbon per pound than a chicken. I always tell them eight-graders, chickens gonna be the death of this planet."

Ladybaby bites her lip and keeps hammering.

Bubblegum sees her squeeze that tender lip, knows he done pissed her off. He goes back to his own yard, watching her sweat in that flower-dress. He'll come by and make her feel sweet later. He really will this time.

Ladybaby goes down to the store, comes back with a cardboard box cluckin in her backseat. She sets it inside the playhouse, opens it, and closes the door. Peakin in through the wire, she sees a flash of green and red and brown feathers. Her four little chickens shoot back and forth across the wire, eyeballin her with them big yellow eyes. She looks down at their feet, sees the spurs, and shudders. Her babies was born with switchblades on their toes.

"Heavengod, now you watch my babies," she say, givin old Heavengod a look like he done broke the dishes.

"I ain't done shit this time," say Heavengod. The sun rolls round backwards and becomes an eye. Heavengod stares down at Ladybaby, say, "Whatever it was, I ain't done it. I been up here this whole time."

"You the disappointingest," Ladybaby tells him. "Nobody said you done nothin. I asked you to watch over my sweet babies down here."

"Oh," say Heavengod, "oh." The suns rolls back around.

Ladybaby pulls up a lawn chair and watches her chickens through the wire. They lose feathers doin so many push-ups and sit-ups, and they scratch out writing on the wall where she can't see, and they speak with bad language. Ladybaby clucks her tongue and worries till she sweats.

Bubblegum watches Ladybaby from his front porch. He wonders if she got a ferret. He wants to go show her how to hold it, how to give it peanut-butter-on-a-cracker, how to drape it around her neck. But he don't want to intrude. He don't want to intrude.

Next morning, Ladybaby wakes from chicken dreams. Has a vase stuffed full of molted chicken feathers on her table. Eats grits with butter while she watch the playhouse sit chicken-filled in the backyard.

Ladybaby say, "I'm gonna let them chickens scratch on the grass while it still wet," and she goes outside to do that thing.

When she gets close to the playhouse, she smell something like nail polish, sees fumes comin out the windows. She hear a police siren and know in her heart that her babies done did something bad.

Ladybaby opens the door. Her chickens scatter to the back of the playhouse, coverin their heads with their wings. Inside, they got her cookpots, her waterhose cut into sections, packs of cold medicine all over the floor, everything wrapped in black tape and bubblin. She cries into her hands. Her babies done built a meth lab.

Police pull up in the yard, and the chickens scatter. Cops is jumpin on chickens, and the chickens cut cop-faces with their feet. Cop draws and shoots a chicken, pops it like a balloon, wet feathers settlin on the ground. The other three drop, wings splayed on the grass.

Ladybaby is cryin so loud, Bubblegum hears it and comes runnin off his porch. "You can't take that Ladybaby's ferret!" he yells at the cops.

Ladybaby cries up to heaven, say, "Heavengod, why didn't you watch my babies?"

The eye of the sun rolls back round and looks at her like he don't remember who she is. Blinks that great god-eye. Heavengod say, "It ain't me. I been up here this whole time."

Ladybaby takes the arm of Corrections Officer, let him lead her to that visitation area.

He say, "Ladybaby, you sure do look fancy in them prison clothes. But we all know it was them chickens built that meth lab. When you gonna come clean?"

"You don't know me," Ladybaby say. "I drink that meth all the time."

Corrections Officer shakes his head, sets her in front of a Plexiglass window.

Her three babies come in and stand on the other side of the glass, lookin down and scratchin at the floor with their feet. They done plucked their arms to show off their muscles and new tattoos. Every one of them got the words, *Chicken Four*, on his shoulder.

"Hey Mama," one of her babies say.

Ladybaby slams her old fist on the window sill, screws her face up, and rubs her forehead. "Why you do it?" she ask.

Chicken One say, "Mama, it's hard being a Banty rooster sold in a pet shop, growin up poor, livin in the city. I'm writin a book all about it."

"And I'm goin round to them high schools talkin to kids," say Chicken Two.

"And I been volunteerin in the community," say Chicken Three.

"What we tryin to say," say Chicken One, "is we tryin to be better people for you, Mama."

Ladybaby cries into her hands. "I love my babies, but I ain't gettin out of prison for years. How my babies gonna grow up right without somebody takin care of em?"

Chicken Three puts his wing on the glass. "Bubblegum been checkin on us two times every day, Mama."

"Bubblegum?" Ladybaby asks.

Chicken Two nods. "He been teachin us how to ride a bicycle. Say if we gonna persist in bein chickens, least we can do is ride a bike to off-set our carbon output."

"He a smart man," say Chicken Three. "Always talkin about carbon. Make me wanna be a chemist, ain't lyin."

"Bubblegum." Ladybaby blushes. "I always did like that Bubblegum."

SPARKS

WHERE THE ELECTRICIAN WENT

IT WAS NIGHT in the nursing home and, his hairy feet slapping the tiles, the electrician raised his long arms over his head and danced in a white gown through the empty hallways. He passed a row of thick windows, the sky black and smooth outside. He twirled past the brooding televisions and hard sofas, breathing in the chemical smell rising from the floors. Every few steps, the electrician would reach up and touch one of the lights, the globe exploding into white luminescence, then move on to the next, a trail of white light snaking from his body to the other end of the nursing home.

Light cutting into their rooms, the residents rolled in their blankets and ground their teeth. They turned away from their doors, but could feel the light on their backs. Thin fingers stabbed call buttons. Hands fumbled around the sides of beds to grab things—oranges, cell phone chargers, bedpans, flower vases, cups of urine—to throw at the dancing man.

Lost in the rapture of electricity, the electrician didn't feel the objects hit his back. He grabbed another bulb, cold in his hand, before heat sizzled through his fingertips and lit it like a match. He felt electricity leave his body and shivered.

The night nurse and her boyfriend brought the electrician down by the cafeteria. Sitting on his back, she told him that he would be sent away in the morning. They strapped him into a wheelchair and rolled him toward his room.

The whole way, he reached for the bulbs above, unable to see or understand anything but the potential for light.

A few weeks before, the electrician had walked out of the trees with a spool of electrical cable on his back and had come to a village in the woods: a dirt lot, clusters of old trucks, dogs and children rolling in the dark under trailers. The people watched him from inside their dim houses. The electrician dropped his heavy spool of cable, stood on top of it, and said, "I've come to bring you light."

A preacher glared at the electrician from the awning of a tin and plywood church. He was wary of silver-headed men carrying cable. He locked the doors and windows, stood alone at the pulpit, and flipped through his Bible searching for passages on the evils of wandering electricians.

The electrician climbed onto the trailer tops and ran a spiderweb of power-lines out over the village. He wired up nightlights in the trees around the town, punched holes through roofs and dropped in metal light sockets on the ends of wire. He called the children to him and gave out light bulbs from his pockets, stacking them like eggs in their small hands. The kids took off their shoes, tied the laces, and threw them onto the lines. The electrician smiled and knew that this was right. It was nearly midnight when everything was ready. Standing in the middle of town, the electrician told the power to come, and the thin houses shuddered when hot yellow light punched them from the inside, pouring from the windows and seeping through cracks in the walls.

Rubbing fists into their eyes, the people ran outside and met in clusters under the alien glow of the nightlights. The electrician opened his arms like a father. "What did you see?" he asked.

They told him. One woman saw that her son didn't love her anymore. Her son saw that he didn't know what love was. One man saw that his children didn't have anything, that he could never work hard enough to give them what they wanted, and that they would always hate him for it.

The electrician put his hands in his jean-pockets and shook his head. He went to another group of people. "You," he said. "What did all of you see?"

One man saw why his wife had left him. A woman saw that she would never be happy here, but was too afraid to go anywhere else. Two parents saw it was their fault that their infant daughter had died. One man saw that the new truck he'd bought was going to break down soon. A woman saw that her husband would never leave her, but that he loved someone else.

The electrician wrapped his arms around himself and stared at the dirt. He passed a hand over his silver head and told them that he was sorry.

The woman who knew she would never be happy told him that the kids were all hiding underneath their beds. They wouldn't come out until their parents had everything cleaned up so they wouldn't have to look at it anymore.

The electrician saw a section of the heavy black cable moving in the wind, an artery disappearing into the trees. "I can make the light go away." He'd never said this before.

"It won't matter."

The electrician went from person to person, demanding they tell him what he could do to fix it.

There was a noise in the trees behind them, and everyone stopped talking. Two wide men in suits came walking out of the woodline and into the porch light. They slapped up meters on every house, wrote out bills and stuffed them into mailboxes.

An older woman walked stiffly out to check her mail, everyone watching. She took out the bill and read it. "We have to pay for this," she told them, "and it's expensive."

The villagers shouted. The company men slapped the electrician on the back. "You've done something no one else could," they told him.

The electrician fell to the ground and rolled onto his side. He shook and kicked up plumes of dust. One of the company men picked him up, folded him over, and tucked him under one arm inside his coat. Cradling the electrician like this, the company men backed away from the village and receded into the trees.

The village sat in a pool of yellow in the middle of the forest. The villagers saw how strange the trees and their houses were in the light, how the shadows were thinner. They looked at each other and could see everything, no secrets between them anymore. They spread apart, not wanting their bodies to touch.

Before the village in the woods, the electrician had set out from the power plant carrying a huge spool of electrical cable on his shoulders and back. He followed the utility poles for most of the day, until they stopped on the edge of a pine forest that went west as far as he could see. The electrician tied his cable into the main line and felt current race through the spool around him. Old nails and screws from the road flew to him and stuck to his skin. He pushed his way into the trees, going places other electricians did not go.

He climbed into the pine branches, wrapping the wire around their trunks, and leapt to the next tree, stringing a line of black cable high off the ground. He began to see houses here and there, chain-link fences and silver butane tanks gleaming in the forest. When he found his way to one of them and knocked, the man set his dogs on the electrician and told him to get the hell out. The electrician put down his burden of cable and kicked the dogs in their sides with his long feet. He chased them all across the yard, kicking them and popping them with his hat, and they cried. The man watched this for a few minutes, never having seen anything like it. The dogs ran underneath the house and barked at the electrician from the dark of the crawlspace.

The man shook his head. "You really believe in this, don't you?"

The electrician wiped the sweat out of his gray eyebrows and said that he did. He spent that afternoon wiring up the man's house. When he was done, the man asked what he should do now. The electrician handed him one round bulb wrapped in tissue paper and said, "Anything in the world." He shouldered his spool of cable again and headed back into the trees.

That night, the electrician was walking though the woods, running into spiderwebs and coarse branches, when he came into a clearing and saw a young woman beside a telescope. He introduced himself and asked what she was doing. The woman said she was looking at the stars. She waved her hand at the sky and began to tell the electrician about Perseus and Cancer, Hydra and Leo. He looked at his shoes. He had been unable to see stars ever since he was a young man. He started telling her about halogens and fluorescents, black-lights and strobe lights. She laughed.

"You can't be serious," she said. "Have you seen Ursa Major? Andromeda?"

He frowned. "Solar cells. LEDs."

They became angry with each other and shouted like this for almost an hour. Virgo. Traffic lights. Lyra. Mood lighting. Orion. Alarm clocks. Taurus. Heating lamps.

"The moon," she shouted, throwing up her arm and pointing at it.

The electrician could feel its weight over his head. It hung, white and thick as a bowl of frozen milk. He had been afraid she would use it against him.

He collected himself. "Movie screens."

She asked him to leave.

Long before astronomers and dark forests, the company men sent the electrician to bring power to a whole city. He spent weeks going in and out of the sewers and train tunnels beneath the streets, pushing along his roll of cable, and wiring the buildings. He went into every home and business, carefully cutting holes in the ceilings and dropping wires down into the old kerosene globes and candle fixtures. A pretty clerk walked by in a black and white checkered dress. The electrician smiled at her and said that she wouldn't have to worry about the smoke anymore. She gave him a tight-lipped smile and kept walking.

That night, the electrician went downtown, stopping by a bench where the streetlight had blown out to tell a man that this was a thing of the past. The man said that he had bigger problems than streetlights.

The electrician was sure that everyone would be grateful once they understood. He imagined the parade they would throw him. There would be a long electric tram, he was sure, with an entire laundromat inside, rows and rows of electric motors humming and spinning their drums. People would hang off the sides dragging raw electrical lines over the street, the current scarring the asphalt. There would be clowns carrying air conditioners on their backs, long extension cords trailing behind them, cooling the street to a perfect seventy-two degrees. He was sure that it would happen just like this.

The electrician turned on the power and watched the lights of the city flare on. It was brighter at first, and parts of the city that had been dark came into view. Then he saw the lights start to change. They shifted to reds and blues and crawled across billboards and signs. There was a sigh from somewhere under his feet, and great machines started to hum in the earth below the city. Things were moving that had never moved before. He walked in and out of every shop, no place in the city dark now. The electrician sat down on a bench, the streetlight burning clear and clean beside him, and watched people move under a sea of colored lights. None of them had noticed.

It was his first job after becoming an electrician, and he was working in a park at night. There were stars burning white above him, so close he could feel their vibrations on the back of his neck, and the electrician loved them as much as he'd ever loved anything. He finished repairing the park's nightlights and cut them back on. They were yellow and murky. The electrician couldn't see the stars anymore because of the light. He walked away into the dark, wandering around on the grass and staring at the sky, but never saw the stars again.

Once, there was a a young man who walked to the power company to apply for the position of electrician. The building was gray, funnel-shaped towers and smokestacks rising up from the flat earth. It was ringed by three fences. Two company men dressed in matching black suits met him at the door and took him inside. There were tests: they handed him a box full of bulbs and made him guess their wattage; they brought him naked wires spitting with current and made him touch them and tell what the voltage was; he was quizzed on every philosopher who had ever written on light and darkness.

After his tests were scored, the company men took him into a small room and removed their suit jackets. They rolled up their sleeves, took him by the shoulders, and dipped him into a tank of electricity. His body compressed and became rigid. A salvo of black and white shapes moved across his eyes. He did not feel so much that he was floating as he felt anchored in space, his body driven like a nail into this point in the universe. The company men pulled him out of the tank and called him brother. The electrician brushed down his hair and rubbed his arms and legs. He knew he was going to do amazing things.

Years before he became an electrician, the boy lived in a narrow wooden house with his parents. His mother was afraid of candles, so whenever they needed light, they stood in front of their windows. The boy brushed his teeth, dressed himself, and did his schoolwork all while looking at the brick street in front of their house. The neighbors tried not to stare.

One day, his father told him that an electrician was coming soon to bring power and light to their home. He went to school that morning and spent the whole day in the library, reading everything he could find on electricity. They didn't allow candles in the school, either, and when a storm passed its black hands over the sun, the boy huddled beside the window with his book open, waiting for lightning flashes so that he could catch another sentence. He read about a man who discovered electricity with a kite and a key, then another man who improved on it with a bigger kite and an entire ring of keys. That man's name had been Jones, and he had put his irradiated keys inside honey jars and sold them to everyone in the county. He kept reading, imagining that having electricity must be like having a giant bolt of lightning standing on top of your house, visible for miles and miles.

After school, he walked to the hardware store in the rain. He told the clerk what he needed and was shown to a shelf filled with light bulbs standing head-down inside egg cartons. Every one of them was different. The boy picked one that was perfectly round and the size of his fist. The clerk wrapped it in tissue paper for him, and the boy took measured steps the entire way home, holding the package to his chest.

All week, the boy stared at the glass globe, turning it so that he could see the filament inside, careful not to shake it too hard or hit it against something. He laid it next to him on his pillow every night and wiped the dust from it every morning.

When an old electrician came, spending hours outside with the grind of saws and the knock of hammers, the boy walked into the living room with his light bulb to wait. The door opened and the old electrician came in. He took the light bulb from the boy, screwed it into a socket in the ceiling, watched the room fill with warm yellow light, and left—like it was nothing.

The boy and his parents stood in the living room together and pressed their faces close to the lit bulb. The longer they stared, the larger it became, seeming to expand into a sun in front of their eyes. It was then that the boy saw that anything was possible.

THE MIRACLES OF BENNY CARR

IN A SEATTLE APARTMENT COMPLEX, there lived a young man named
Benny Carr. The neighbors on his floor had no idea what he did for a living,
nor did they know his hobbies, which gym he preferred, or whether or not he
was single. They invited him to their weekend cookouts, but Benny never came.
After forty days and forty nights of this, his neighbors gathered one morning
and decided to confront him. So they surrounded his door, beat on it with their
fists, and yelled for him to come out.

The door opened. Benny blinked and wiped his eyes, his shirt wrinkled
and hair standing up.

"Am I parked wrong?" he asked. "Did I forget to pay my rent?"

Lily, a woman who'd had her eye on Benny ever since he'd moved in,
who watched him come and go at all hours, who had dreamed up what their
life together would be like and even named their hypothetical children and
three cats, but who had grown angry at him for resisting her invitations to the
building events, her heart now already thinking of hypothetical divorce because
of his selfishness, stepped forward.

"You will explain yourself, Benny Carr," she told him. "Why do you not
come to our cookouts? Why do you stay up so late playing music in your one
bedroom apartment? Why has your bicycle been broken and chained to the
stairwell for six weeks? It is because you have no love for your fellow man."

Benny looked on the crowd, come to him with stern faces and wearing white, collared shirts. He opened the door wider, letting daylight fall on an overflowing trash can, the flickering face of the television, a floor sticky with spilled soda.

"I'm more full of love than any of you know," he told them. "My doctor has remarked on the size and strength of my heart, and my optometrist on the kindness and honesty of my eyes. I will prove the depth of my love to you all."

"How will you do that, Benny Carr?" Lily asked, the crowd nodding behind her. "What can you do?"

Benny looked around his kitchen, his eyes settling on the stacks of Styrofoam take-out boxes on his counter. "Come outside your apartments at this time every morning for the next three days. Don't come out earlier, not even to check your mail. Then you will understand."

The other tenants agreed and left, only Lily staying behind. She held up five fingers. "Five times have I invited you to a cookout, Benny Carr. And five times have I made a spinach dip, and five times have I personalized your invitation. What could you do to prove that you have a heart?"

Benny led her back down the flight of stairs to her door. "Come outside tomorrow at eleven, and you will see the miracle of my love."

Benny went back into his apartment, threw his shirt into the dryer until it was fresh, and put it back on. Late in the evening, he unlocked his bike from the stairwell and fixed the broken chain while his neighbors watched from their windows. Years later, people would remember this as his first miracle. Benny Carr rode his bicycle twelve blocks to the Super Panda, a Chinese buffet. Here, Benny ate one plate of food for every tenant in his building, all one hundred and six of them. A line of waitresses stretched from his table to the kitchen, the carpet below his feet sticky with soy sauce and spotted with rice. Then he bought a bag of Chinese fortune cookies, broke and ate them, and collected the fortunes.

Benny pedaled home with his aching gut, found scotch tape in his apartment, and taped a fortune to every door of the building. Then he went back home, pulled a blanket over himself on the couch, and fell asleep.

The tenants came out the next morning at eleven, just as Benny had instructed, and found the fortunes taped to their doors. They scoffed at Benny Carr and said that he was a selfish man and a fool.

"I can go to Panda Express and get this any day of the week," a man said.

"And I got this same fortune once at Fat Panda," said Lily. She sighed and wondered how she could have ever loved a man like him.

They were gathered on the balcony, wondering what they would do, when one of the tenants came forward in her underwear, a lovely young man on her arm. "I met him last night and missed my alarm to go to work this morning," she said. "When we got up, I found this on my door." She handed them her fortune. It read, *A new friend helps you break out of an old routine.*

An older woman found dozens of checks in her mailbox, made out to her from a German pharmaceutical company. Her fortune promised wealth.

Everyone marveled at the size of their blessings. They stuck the fortunes to their shirts and walked the stairwells together, showing what kind Benny Carr had blessed them with.

Lily showed everyone her fortune, *Love Is At Your Hands Bee Glad And Hold On To It,* which she told everyone was the greatest of them all, a sign that Benny truly loved her.

One woman saw that she would discover her hidden talents. A man that the troubles he had now would pass quickly away. Someone read that he would enjoy good health and be surrounded by luxury. Good fortune multiplied by one hundred and six had been Benny Carr's, but his desire to prove his love was so great that he gave it all up, keeping no good thing for himself. By that afternoon, everyone on the block had heard of Benny Carr.

The next night, Benny went back to the Super Panda and did the same, and again the night after, coming home sticky with General Tso's chicken, his breath stinking of eggrolls, and cheap buffet sushi working evil in his gut. He had sought fortune and given it up for his neighbors three times.

After his work was done, Benny Carr chained his bicycle to the stairwell, went back into his apartment, and fell asleep on his couch. He was sure that in the morning, the tenants would come to beg his forgiveness. But the food had been bad, and Benny Carr became sick. He vomited for hours, holding his stomach, and he finally died amidst the filth of his couch cushions just before eleven o'clock on the third day.

The tenants came outside and found their third day of blessings, talking excitedly to one another about what a generous man Benny Carr was and how they shouldn't disturb him in the future. Everyone was pleased with their blessings—good health, happiness, and love—except for Lily. She had learned that a man had received the same fortune which Benny had given her on the first day. When she tried to take it from him, telling the man that it must be a mistake, two others came forward and told Lily that they also had received this fortune, but they had hidden it from her so that she wouldn't be broken-hearted.

Embarrassed, Lily went back into her apartment and sat on her bed. She realized now that Benny Carr's love was not for her alone, but for all mankind in equal measure, and she wept bitterly into her throw pillows until her throat ached and her makeup ran and the fabric of the pillows was stained and ruined.

Three days later, Benny Carr's body was still in his room and no one had come to check on him. Lily made more invitations for a cookout in the park, but she could not invite Benny, afraid that he might come and see how badly she was hurt.

But on the day of the cookout, Benny was resurrected into a new body, a vessel of pure love and good fortune. He stepped off the Amtrak in glory and light, and Benny went straight to the park where the tenants were having their party, carrying a dozen boxes of Chinese take-out with him. They ate from the boxes and gathered around him, slapping his back and thanking him for the good fortunes. Lily kept away, feeling foolish for thinking he might love only her and trying not to cry as she watched him play Frisbee and pet dogs with his neighbors.

Benny ate their hot dogs and drank their beer, walking among them as a resurrected being, though they did not know it. Finally, when he could stand it no more, he called for everyone to come listen. He raised his arms and, like throwing back a sheet, revealed his true form.

The tenants fell down in awe before Benny Carr. His skin was made of strips of glowing fortunes. Beneath, radiant red love pumped through his veins. He spoke in a voice that rattled like hundreds of bicycle chains, and the smell of sesame chicken was his breath.

"This body you see is of the spirit," he said. "Three days ago, I was poisoned with bad sushi and died in my apartment, but none of you came to check on me. You do not deserve my kindness, nor my fortunes."

The tenants all began talking at once, afraid that Benny would take away the blessings he had given them. He held up a hand and silenced the multitude.

"Do not be afraid that I will take from you. For I am not He Who Takes, but He Who Gives. I gladly give you the fortunes, and this I give too: my corpse, triple-locked inside my apartment, empty shell of flesh and salmonella. My body will foul up the apartment complex, and the scent of it will bring health inspectors down on you, and all of you will have to move out in less than a week. You will be scattered across the city, some of you back to the homes of your parents."

His neighbors begged Benny to forgive them, following him all the way to the Amtrak station, but he would not listen. There, he boarded a train to Chicago and vanished from their lives forever. Only Lily managed to get on the train and follow him to his holy city. She searched for Benny Carr in every Chinese buffet, under swinging yellow lights and between narrow aisles of reheated food, but she could not find him. She asked people if they knew Benny Carr, and when they said no, she told them about him and his miracles.

That the crumb-covered fortunes in their hands and, indeed, all crumb-covered fortunes were the blessings of Benny Carr. That they should be thankful for everything, but not desire Benny Carr for themselves, because his love was for all mankind. She put her hand to her breast and told them that she knew this better than anyone. Their hearts would only get broken if they tried to keep him.

THE INSULTING OF WARLORD REISHI

THIS STORY IS STILL TOLD in the airports of Texas, how one day the warlords Yatshiro and Reishi boarded flight 293 Austin to Los Angeles. They moved like bulls down the jetway, pushing aside the other passengers while dragging rolling suitcases and thumping iron canes. Ducking into the plane and searching for their seats, the two men stepped out of the aisle to allow a lovely stewardess to pass. Her hair was short and dark, her skin almond-white. As she glided down the aisle, they could feel her every step in their skin. Both men were taken with her.

Reishi said the woman was like his mother. He shoved his suitcase and cane into the overhead compartment.

Yatshiro said that this was not so, and that the stewardess was more like a girl he knew in his village who collected lake flowers and sang while she listened to R&B on her headphones.

Reishi waved for Yatshiro to stop, reminding him that he'd heard all this before. His friend had given the same honor to their last waitress.

Yatshiro insisted that he always meant what he said. He stowed his luggage beside his friend's, their iron canes clinking together in the compartment. The two men compared their tickets and realized they were sitting two rows apart.

Reishi remarked that for a short time they must journey alone.

Yatshiro, completing the proverb, said that a man always does.

They took their seats. The plane pulled out from the gate, accelerated down the runway, and lifted into the air.

Reishi could barely see his friend from where he sat crammed against the window. They'd only been in the air a few moments when he felt pressure on his arm. The man seated beside him was using his armrest.

Reishi raised one of his great fists and struck the man in the chest.

The man yelled, asking what the hell was going on. He stabbed the call button and kept repeating himself, demanding an explanation.

Reishi refused to speak the barbaric tongue if he could avoid it. He gave the man a look of warning and went back to looking out his window.

A few moments later, the man's arm touched Reishi's again. Furious, Reishi was of no mind to wait for the proverbial third offense. He raised his fist again. The man wailed and shrank into his seat. Reishi struck him on the chest and over the head, cursing his peasant manners, until the man bailed out of his chair and went to hide in the lavatory. He stayed there for the remainder of the flight.

The lovely stewardess came and asked if everything was okay. Reishi could only smile.

The flight was a long one. With several seat rows between them, Reishi and Yatshiro discussed a song that they had heard on the radio. They bellowed over their seats at one another, yelling the verses of pop music as they remembered them and arguing over what the song meant. Yatshiro grew obstinate, refusing to turn and listen, so Reishi pelted him with M&Ms to get his attention. The people seated around Yatshiro ducked and made murmurs against him.

A third time the lovely stewardess appeared, asking the men to be quiet and to respect the other passengers. Yatshiro and Reishi swore themselves to silence for the rest of the flight and promised that they would forgive the other passengers for their rudeness. The stewardess walked away.

For the next hour, both warlords stayed in their seats and did not debate songs or poetry. They did not hit the other passengers, even when a particularly ugly child would not stop staring at Yatshiro.

The flight went on this way until Reishi became conscious of a great injustice. Yatshiro in his aisle seat had full view of the lovely stewardess at her work. He had been able to observe her beauty this entire time, no doubt comparing her large eyes to those of his remembered lake girl. Reishi, however, was against the window and could only see quick flashes of her as she walked by. His thirst only increased, while Yatshiro glutted himself on the girl's image.

He checked his watch and decided that this had gone on long enough.

Reishi called to his friend and asked him to switch seats.

Yatshiro pretended not to hear, but Reishi was persistent, until his friend asked him why.

Reishi said that Yatshiro's place was a wealthy one, and it would be unlawful for him to hold it while his friend was in poverty for the entire flight.

Yatshiro replied that fate makes lords and paupers as it would, though he agreed with Reishi's estimation that he was quite rich.

Reishi countered that what was in the hands of men to decide could not rightly be called fate.

Yatshiro only laughed and told his friend to calm himself. He promised to share tales of his fortune with Reishi at the flight's end.

This was not acceptable.

Resihi yelled and stood up from his seat. The passengers removed their earphones to see what the commotion was about this time. Reishi teetered into the aisle as the plane shifted, then jerked open the overhead compartment. He dropped his suitcase into the aisle and zipped it open.

Yatshiro asked what this foolishness was.

Reishi swore to slay Yatshiro for his villainy. He asked his friend how highly would he regard fate when it planted a blade in his throat.

Incensed, Yatshiro rose and grabbed his luggage as well.

The two men shed their suitcoats and pulled off their undershirts, tossing them into their seats. From the rolling suitcases, they unpacked their brightly lacquered armor. For Yatshiro, his armaments were yellow, his helmet etched with the designs of a bird. Reishi was a dragon in green armor accented with gold, his helmet horned and fierce. The two men brought down their canes, twisted the heads off of them, and pulled free gleaming swords. The sound of metal sliding free of iron cases shivered through the cabin. Below the armor, they wore pressed slacks and Armani shoes.

Everyone was surprised when it began. There was no taunting, no deliberation as to whether or not they would go through with it. Such men had their killing rules in place at all times. Once insulted, neither had a doubt.

Yatshiro rushed forward, bringing his sword across in fast chops, making an X in the air. Reishi met him, his own bright sword singing against his friend's. Yatshiro was spun off balance and accidentally beheaded one of the other passengers as he tried to keep his feet. The woman's ponytailed head dropped down into her lap. None of her family having the decency to move it, it rested there for the remainder of the flight.

The warlords collided in the tilting aisle, their blades lashing out and licking against armor, stripping lacquer and squealing as they came apart. The seat-tops around them fell away, their stuffing and dingy vinyl scattering like chopped weeds. The passengers howled like pigs when an errant cut found them. They bled and piled themselves against the sides of the plane.

The plane fell, and oxygen masks dropped, hanging in the air like a forest. The warlords sliced through them to find each other. The pilot screamed something over the intercom that no one could understand, and the plane spun violently. The warlords fought and laughed, climbing the walls and following the curve of the plane. The passengers cowered and cried, trying to get away, but they were wedged in too tightly. The flinched under the hard shoes and sharp blades, their soft bodies trampled and pierced. They died by the score.

Reishi and Yatshiro battled until sweat iced their dented armor and the plane was in steep descent. Droplets of blood pulled away from the floor and struck the roof of the cabin, rain falling upward. People were dumped over their ruined seat-backs and lay entwined on the floor in peaceful heaps. The warlords stopped. The beauty of the scene dawned on the men at the same time, their swords lowering.

Reishi admitted that he may have been childish.

Yatshiro, flicking a viscous rope of blood onto the floor, said that it was he who had been childish, unwilling to share his obvious bounty.

They wiped their blades on the flannel jacket of the nearest passenger and embraced, begging one another's forgiveness. Most of coach lay carved up at their feet, broken spars of chair surrounding them. They found their suitcases in the rubble and repacked their armor, sheathed their blades, and pulled their dark jackets back on. Saddest of all to them, the lovely stewardess had locked herself in the cockpit when the fighting had begun and did not emerge the rest of the flight.

The plane made a rough landing and stalled out on the tarmac. They opened the emergency exit, and the warlords Reishi and Yatshiro disembarked alone.

When the Plumber Drank the Ghosts

THE PLUMBER HAD BEEN HIRED to exorcise the house of its ghosts. He parked his van on the side of the street and looked up at the house, all weathered gray wood, balconies, and wrap-around porches. It had been a bar once, before it had been sold as a house and the haunting had started. He grabbed a flat metal toolbox and began walking up the hill.

On the phone earlier, the owner had told the plumber that she'd already called a priest, an exterminator, and a weatherman, but none of them could get rid of the ghosts. The plumber said that he could always take a look.

It was morning, and bees lifted and sank into the thick green, the plumber's thin legs swishing through stalks of grass. Dandelions broke into yellow, bobbing in the wind, and dust of pollen and grass seed coated the world. The plumber was a wire of a man with a sagging black mustache, tired eyes, and a bent back. His right hand was always twisting, working a wrench that wasn't there. The sun was full above him, warming his arms. He smiled at the clump of irises growing by the door and felt good about things.

The door was unlocked, and he went through the dark foyer, stopping just inside the living room. He stood quietly for a long time and did not breathe, listening to the soft flutter of newspapers. Across couches, chairs, and scattered barstools—in the wide space that had once been the main room of the bar—some thirty ghosts read newspapers and drank coffee in the pale light coming in through the windows. Their flesh was fish-like, silvery and wet, and they stank of alcohol. They wore flannel shirts and some wore hats, and they blinked their big eyes and traded papers and magazines occasionally. When the plumber walked in, the ghosts all looked up at him for a moment, then went back to their coffee and reading.

The plumber fixed himself a cup of coffee. On the bar, three coffee pots, overlapping coffee rings, empty packets of creamer, and one very dirty spoon. "Well, you all probably know why I'm here," he told them.

The ghosts watched him, but said nothing.

"We should get to know each other first. I'm Henry. What do you want to know? Ask me anything."

The ghosts steamed from their mouths and ears, their voices squealing like kettles. One of them put its arm around the plumber.

"You got a girlfriend, sugar?" the ghost asked.

The other ghosts shook their heads. "That's bar talk," one said. "This isn't the place for that anymore."

Henry laughed and pulled at his plumber's collar. "It's complicated."

"Do you watch baseball?" one asked.

"Sometimes I do."

The ghosts nudged one another. Finally they were getting somewhere.

The ghost said, "I like Little League games, myself. Do you have kids who play?"

Another nodded. "Now that's more appropriate."

The plumber started to speak, but he didn't know what to say. "Maybe I should just get started," he said.

He downed his coffee and walked upstairs to look at the rest of the house.

The ghosts watched the plumber leave the room and wondered what they had done wrong. They remembered a time when the bar had been full of people and no one noticed them standing on the edges of the room, finishing off empty bottles, sucking in the cigarette smoke and the music, collecting beads of moisture from tables and floors and lips. They had pulled used napkins out of trash bins, unfolded them in their hands, and read what was inside: lipstick prints, names and phone numbers, food stains, scraps of poems or architectural diagrams, dirty drawings. These they had tucked inside their coats to fill where their hearts had been. That was a long time ago.

The plumber made his way through the house, wandering into bathrooms and kitchens, testing every faucet he saw. He wasn't happy with what he'd found. There was almost no water pressure, and the upstairs sink didn't work. When he turned on the downstairs shower, instead of water, the sound of a neighbor's television poured out: buzzing, applause, the crisp-voiced announcer. Henry stared into the spout in wonder. Things were much worse than ghosts.

He pulled back boards so that he could get in behind the shower to find out what had gone so wrong, when three ghosts came into the bathroom.

"What are you doing?" they asked. "Aren't you going to try to make us leave?"

Henry pointed at the shower-head, strange sounds coming from it. "Someone is watching *Wheel of Fortune*," he said. He found a nest of coaxial cable all mixed up in the plumbing and went outside to follow it. The ghosts watched him from the windows.

The plumber walked across the yard and rang the neighbor's doorbell. He spoke to the woman who answered briefly, then moved down to the next house and did the same. House after house, asking each person, "Are you watching *Wheel of Fortune* reruns this morning?"

An hour later, Henry came back from the neighbors, his clothes damp and dirty. The ghosts handed him a fresh cup of coffee at the door, and he thanked them.

"I don't understand how things got so bad," he said.

"We're sorry," said one of the ghosts.

Henry's hand was twitching. "No. The plumbing. The neighbor told me that every weekday at six, if she turned to channel 3, water would come pouring out of her television. It's been that way for ten years."

Henry carried his toolbox into the kitchens and bathrooms, working on the plumbing until it was dark. The whole time, the ghosts crowded around him and asked questions.

"You ever been married?" a ghost asked.

The plumber frowned and asked for his pipe-wrench. "Everything under here needs to be replaced."

A ghost handed the wrench to him. "Do you live in town?"

The plumber told the ghost to hand him a roll of stiff cable which he began using to snake out the drain. "Nasty clog down there."

Henry fixed the plumbing as best he could, his clothes damp and smelling of drains, and went back out to his van. It was dark out, the lit windows filled with a cluster of ghosts watching him. He got a six-pack of beer out of an ice chest in his van—what he always did after a job—and took it inside. He sat down on the sofa, all the ghosts gathered around him and staring at the six cans in his lap.

"I've been thinking about adopting a little girl from China," a ghost said. "I've always wanted a daughter."

The plumber sighed. "I have to find a way to get rid of you." He popped open one of the cans.

The ghosts felt the fumes of beer rise in the room, molecules of alcohol dispersing in the air and striking their silvery skin like hammers. They remembered how the bar had been before, the crowds of people, the whiskey smell that hung in the air, the things they used to find on the floor or forgotten in bathroom stalls and show one another, everything they had lost.

The nearest three ghosts grabbed the edge of the can—the plumber hanging tight to it—and pushed their way inside the tiny mouth. Their clothes, newspapers, and coffee cups fell in a heap by the couch, and they were gone.

They had lost themselves in a sea of cheap beer, their silvery bodies dissolving into the liquid. The can felt heavier in Henry's hand. He drank it, the cold burning his throat. He opened another.

Again, the ghosts closest to him shoved their way inside. The plumber drank slowly, the metal edge of the can stinging his lip. He went on like this until he was a little drunk and all the ghosts were gone. They filled his belly and moved through his blood, circulating mournfully through his brain. He began to remember all the mistakes he'd made: clogs only partially removed, leaky faucets he'd given up on, illegitimate children he'd fathered all over town and never visited. He was ashamed of everything he had ever done.

That night, drunk and body heavy with the cold weight of ghosts, the plumber climbed back into his van and drove from house to house. He went to moonlit doorways where he'd had final kisses, the dark landings where he'd taken his last times and last last times. He beat on the doors of old lovers and demanded to be let inside so that he could fix things the way a plumber ought to.

They let him in, seeing ghosts in his eyes. Henry pulled out clogs of hair he'd given up on and fixed sinks that had been dribbling for years. The women and their husbands watched him with bleary eyes, not understanding his slurred words or the clumps of drain-filth he held up to them. He went into the bedrooms of his forgotten children, took them from their beds, and lined them up in the backseat of his van, one after another.

Railroad Burial

SIXTEEN DAYS AFTER the engineer died, all the locomotives on the line filled with black smoke. It rose like a ghost out of the fireboxes and went hissing through the compartments. All trains were stopped until their coal burnt out. Afterward, the soot was crusted black on everything, oily and smelling like meat, and all the engineers cursed the fireman for what he had done.

Two years before the engineer died, the fireman found a rail rider clinging to the end of the caboose. The man's body was bent double over the railing in the cold rain. The wind had ripped his clothes apart, and they dragged behind him like old skins. The fireman went to the cab, the engineer wrapped in coal-dusted denim and eating cigarette after cigarette while he watched the gauges. The fireman told him about the dead man, and they stopped the train. They took the rail rider's frozen body, scooped out some rocks under the track, and shoved him under. The engineer wrapped the man's fingers around the metal rails. "This is railroad burial," the engineer said. "We have to hold the track up forever." He ate a few more cigarettes and they got back on the train. The rail rider braced the track under them.

One year before the engineer died, he found the fireman out on the running board. The moon was glutted with light. The engineer stank from whiskey and nightmares. Underneath them, the wheels of the train clicked over the fingers of the dead men holding up the track. The engineer grabbed the fireman's shirt in his fists. "Swear you won't put me under there when I die, or I'll kill you."

The day the engineer died, the others came in their coal-blacked denim, offered grease for his engine, and ate the last of his cigarettes. They asked the fireman if he knew what to do, and he said he did. The fireman shoved out the ice and stones and placed the engineer under the tracks. He wrapped the man's strong dead fingers around the rails and walked away from his promise.

Fourteen days after the engineer died, the fireman cowered under nightmares sleeping and waking. He couldn't take the sound of the wheels cutting across dead fingers anymore. He stole a railcar and rode all up and down the tracks, but he couldn't tell the engineer from any of the other sun-whitened dead. The fireman peeled back their fingers, stacked them like logs on the railcar, and rode away. The rails sagged weakly beneath him.

Fifteen days after the engineer died, the fireman was cold and alone. He needed to hide the dead before the engineers found him. He rode back into the station one night, and working in the dark of the railyard, he stuffed the bodies deep into the coal chutes until they were all gone, until his throat was filled with soot, until it was morning.

Sixteen days after the engineer died, the trains loped back toward the station on the sagging track, crusted over with soot and stinking like meat. The fireman hiding in the woods saw the rails warping and spreading apart. He knew the trains would slide off and pile on the trackside, their metal hulls pressing engineers and firemen to death. He ate his last cigarette and crawled underneath the track. Grabbing the rails in each hand, he held them together and listened to the black trains shrieking forward out of the night. He squeezed the rails and wept. No matter what happened, it would be his fault.

HOW THE WEATHERMAN
BEAT THE STORM

CARLOS FINALLY MADE UP HIS MIND to speak to the lovely weather girl. He'd seen her around the TV station, going from the studio to her office, from her office to the ladies' room, occasionally in the break room or lobby. The carpet crackled with static under her feet wherever she went, the coffee pot boiled at her passing, and the fluorescent lights trembled as she walked beneath them. Back then, he'd thought nothing of it, sure that these things happened only because she was so beautiful.

He worked transporting camera equipment for the TV station. He liked to tell people that he was a cameraman, because cameraman was a name that meant something, but Carlos only drove the van for the real camera crew. He loaded and unloaded their equipment, laughed at their jokes, brought them food on long days when they were filming. And because he was a little heavier than he wanted to be, and short, and—no matter what he told his roommates—only a van driver after all, Carlos had only watched the weather girl from afar.

It was cigarettes that brought them together. Carlos walked down the hallway, trying to take up as little space as possible, pulling his Marlboros out of his pocket and sticking one in his mouth. As he passed her office on his way to the balcony where smoking was permitted, she looked up, all wide eyes and curly blond hair piled on her head. How he must have looked to her, Carlos thought, short and wide, a bent cigarette hanging from his mouth.

He hurried to the door and stepped outside. Looking back, he saw that she was following him: gray suit, hands at her sides, eyes on him. Carlos went out on the balcony and pressed himself against the wall. The small, southern California town lay spread out before him, green and low. A city ordinance mandated that no building be higher than three stories, so from the balcony of the news station, Carlos could see everything. Palm trees climbing into the sky, ball fields dotted with children, the snaking asphalt of suburban cul-de-sacs.

The weather girl came out and walked right up to him, sunlight breaking through the clouds and falling on her face. Carlos was afraid that he had done something to offend her.

"Can I have one of those?" She pointed to the cigarette.

Was her name Laura? He wanted to ask, but he was embarrassed that he didn't know. She had always been the weather girl to him, someone important.

"Sure," Carlos said. He handed her the pack. "Of course." A pretty woman could ask for anything, he thought, and you understood that she owed you nothing. It was enough that she spoke to you.

They stood and smoked in silence for a time. The wind ruffled her rolled shirt sleeves, spun the loose ends of her hair, dispersed the smoke from her cigarette.

Carlos had seen her around the building and had wanted her for five months. Now, the two of them were alone on the balcony. He had a cigarette's time to talk to her.

"So are you a meteorologist?" he asked.

She laughed. "No. They can only name what I am."

Carlos nodded, not understanding. But he was determined to keep the conversation going. If he only talked to her, then he might go home tonight feeling as though he had done something.

"So weather girl is fine then?"

She nodded.

"Do you like doing it?"

She smiled, the sun glinting on her teeth. "It's better than it used to be. Once, they'd have burned me at the stake."

Again he did not know how to respond. The weather girl stood in her gray blazer and skirt, her cigarette almost finished. Carlos badly needed to say something that would make her like him.

"I always wanted to be a weatherman," he said, though this had never been true. "How did you get your start?"

She looked at him very seriously, the cigarette burnt down to the filter and smoldering between her fingers. The wind picked up on the balcony, hurling leaves, twigs, and green insects against the glass windows behind them.

"You really want to be a weatherman?" she asked. All her attention was focused on him.

Carlos looked into her eyes and knew that he could say nothing but yes to her.

"All my life," he said. "I've always wanted to be a weatherman."

At those words, a thunderclap came from the west, a storm building along the coast. It started to rain slightly, the drops small and cold.

Carlos laughed. "Didn't you say a few hours ago that it was going to be sunny today?"

"I can change my mind if I want," she said.

He swallowed. The rain seeped through his second-hand sports coat.

"What's happening?" he asked.

"There's a storm sitting on your back," she told him. "It will hound you from one end of California to the other. When you can make it go away, on that day you will be a weatherman."

And with that, the weather girl wished him luck, walked back into the building, and returned to her office.

§

Carlos went home that night to the old house he rented with four others. He stood at the window and watched the storm building outside. By evening, thunderclaps rattled the windows constantly, and water had risen to cover his bottom step. His roommates pushed the sofa and TV out of the way. They took one of the doors off its hinges and made a ping-pong table of it, asking him to play. But Carlos only stared out at the rain while the tiny plastic ball clicked back and forth behind him, thinking of the weather girl and the things she had said.

By morning, the storm had gotten even stronger, crashing against the walls of the house. The hairs on Carlos's arms were standing up, and he shocked himself every time he touched a doorknob, his fingers stinging. He put pot-holders on his hands and fumbled through the house.

The TV station called and said that they needed him to drive the weather girl around town to cover the storm. But he was afraid of her and what she had done to him. He said that he was sorry, but he was quitting. He was only a van driver after all. He didn't have much to lose.

Over the next few days, the storm pursued him. Its lightning flashed in his windows and its thunder shook the house, making it impossible to sleep. He wrapped a yellow raincoat around himself and went out to buy groceries. The wind knocked him down and rolled him up against the side of the house, where he slipped in the water and could hardly get up again. By the time he'd gotten home, he was coughing and shivering, a cold piece of the storm settled down into his lungs.

His roommates found Carlos coughing on the couch, pot-holders on his hands, the raincoat on his back, every hair on his body standing up. He had been like this for days.

"What's become of you?" they asked him.

"I have pneumonia," said Carlos.

There was a television in the corner, and he kept it tuned to his old TV station. When the weather girl appeared, he shushed his roommates, hoping she would announce that the storm would finally end.

"Bad weather continues over downtown," she said, "flash flooding has closed roads and ruined people's homes. But the rest of the city is nothing but sunshine." She smiled into the camera, and Carlos began to cry into his pot-holders.

"Give me the phone," he demanded.

One of his roommates handed it to him.

Carlos called the TV station and asked to be connected to the weather girl's office.

She picked up and said, "You can't beat the storm by hiding from it."

"Please take it away," he said. He fell into coughing again, holding the phone against his chest. "I didn't mean what I said."

"It's too late not to say it," she told him. "The storm is on your back."

Carlos pushed through the rain and collapsed inside his car, determined to go see the weather girl. But his car battery was dead. He went back inside, shivering and soaked, and fell again on the couch. The fabric was the color of mustard, and if he wrapped the raincoat tightly around himself, he wondered if he might sink down into it and disappear for good.

When he woke up, his roommates were shoving all the furniture into the hallway to make room for a birthday party. Carlos found his couch swept out of the room. Someone threw him a packet of balloons.

"Be useful. Blow these up."

Carlos gave a ragged cough and looked at his roommates helplessly, but they insisted. He pulled his pot-holders off, edging away from the metal lamp that had been shoved into the hallway beside him, and tore open the package.

He pulled in a huge gulp of air, letting his lungs stretch as wide as they could go, put the balloon to his mouth, and blew. He could feel something cold slide past his lips, his mouth going numb. The balloon swelled with black clouds, writhing with hairline arcs of lightning, the sound of tiny rain striking the rubber sides. Carlos held the balloon and stared at it for a long time, the storm thrashing within.

When his roommates saw, they were thrilled. They took the balloon and tossed it into the air, the storm drifting up to bounce along the ceiling.

They covered Carlos in packets of balloons. "Do all of them," they said.

He inflated balloons until his cheeks were stretched sore and his chest ached, falling into coughing fits. His balloons collected along the ceiling of the house, a hundred tiny storms bumping into each other, flashing with angry light. His roommates turned off all the lights in the house, spreading the balloons around like lamps.

He lay on the couch and slept through the noise of the party, his head aching. But he breathed easier now that he'd gotten some of the storm out of his lungs. He sat up and rubbed his head, knowing that he had to make a decision.

When everyone had gone to bed, Carlos went to the door and looked out. He watched the wind run trash back and forth over the asphalt. His town had suffered enough, and he hadn't been outside in over a month. He would try to fight it, he decided. Even if he didn't know how.

He walked into the storm and toward his car, the rain beating him across the back, his shoes soaked. By the time he made it to the door, dropping his keys twice and having to look for them in the dark, he remembered that the battery was still dead. Above, a ragged spear of lightning split the sky in half. The hairs all over his body twitched and stood up. Carlos opened the hood of his old Volkswagen, rubbed his palms together until his fingers tingled, and grabbed his car battery in both hands. He could feel electrical current moving through his arms.

He climbed back into his car and turned the key, the engine jumping to life. Panting, Carlos leaned over the steering wheel, water dripping down his face and pooling on the floor mat. He had not slept in weeks, but he wasn't tired. He could feel heat and air rolling through his chest, energy in his arms and hands. Carlos laughed and wondered if this was what it was like to be a weatherman.

Pointing his Volkswagen to the east, Carlos drove through hail and thunder, wind and rain. When his windows blew in, laying glass in his lap, he buttoned his yellow raincoat up to the neck. The storm dented the top of the car and soaked his skin until he was clammy and itched from the top of his scalp to the pale bottoms of his feet. He drove straight into the Mojave Desert, towing the storm behind him, determined to see it die of thirst.

Far away at his old TV station, a team of meteorologists watched the storm slide across their radar. It followed the interstate on its way east, stopping over the desert. They watched their screens and chewed their pens, trying to understand.

Carlos left his car at a state rest stop and continued on foot to where storms go to die. He walked for hours, the moisture burning off in the hot air, but the wind would not go away. It twirled columns of dust and sent sand flying into his eyes and teeth. Carlos wandered between cacti and large, smooth stones. The sun scorched him pink, and he crawled into the shade of a boulder to rest.

In the desert, Carlos became hungry. He walked until he saw a line of ants navigating the spines of a cactus and began to eat of them freely, following the trail back to its mound. Carlos found that ants were the most numerous things in the world, and this was how he sustained himself. Dust devils clawed at him. Wind and sand made his skin rough. His raincoat bleached almost white in the sun. For a time, it was only he and the lizards among the stones and the cacti, eating ants together and running into one another at night. He started to forget all about the weather girl who had cursed him.

Then others came.

Carlos awoke to find a group of people dressed in church clothes standing around him. He knew that they must be having a picnic at one of the state parks close by. He hadn't meant to wander so near the main road.

Carlos picked himself up and started to leave, but the people in their white shirts, floral dresses, and suspenders followed.

"Who are you?" they asked. "Are you homeless?"

Carlos supposed that he was, but he didn't want to say so. He kept walking, rubbing his tangled beard and wishing he had brought a razor with him when he'd run away from the world.

"Are you a hermit?" they asked. "Are you a holy man in those white robes?"

He looked down at the raincoat and gave a dry laugh, hardly any sound coming out. One of the church people handed him a bottle of water.

Carlos drained it and handed it back. "Yes," he said, "I am a holy man. If you see my roommates, tell them that."

Carlos stumbled off into the desert, the wind pushing him along, and thought that he was rid of them for good. But the next night, they found him again.

He awoke to find them gathered on their knees, a dozen unhappy people. They brought him snacks from the gas station down the road. He wondered what they would ask in return.

"If you are a holy man, you can perform miracles."

Carlos swallowed the Gatorade and ate the Slim Jim they had given him.

"I'm only out here because I lied to impress the weather girl," he said.

The people nodded, but they did not go. Now that they had decided he was a holy man, they weren't letting him out of their sight.

He sighed a long and windy sigh. "You want a miracle. Hand me your cell phones."

They pulled the phones from their pockets and lay them on the ground. Carlos cupped the phones in his palms, watching the battery gauges fill. One by one, the phones beeped to announce that they were finished charging, and Carlos handed them back.

"What else can you do?" they asked.

Carlos took them to a vending machine at the rest stop and shorted it out with a touch, causing it to dispense dozens of sodas. He gave each of them two.

"Satisfied?" he asked.

"We've heard of an electrician who can do things like this," they said. "These aren't miracles."

While Carlos stared at them helplessly, a dust devil crept up behind him and blew sand down his shirt. Angry, he waved his arms, knocking the dust devil away from him. It rolled back, and Carlos threw himself into the middle of it, punching and swearing until it drifted away. He panted, and the people handed him one of their sodas, impressed with how he had fought the wind.

Knowing that he could get his hands on the storm now, Carlos performed miracles in the desert. He pulled clouds over them to give shade, steadied the wind so they could fly kites, kept up a cool breeze, and shocked anyone who touched him.

One day, Carlos and his followers had wandered close to the rest stop again. He went to get change out of his car, then to the payphone. First he called his roommates to tell them that he was a preacher now. Next he called the TV station and asked to speak to the lovely weather girl.

"Hello Carlos," she said.

He blushed to hear her say his name, frustrated that he wanted her still, even after all that had happened.

"I've done it," he told her. "The wind does as I say. I'm a weatherman now."

"You still haven't gotten the storm off your back. Until then, you are nothing." She hung up.

Carlos slammed down the phone and went back to his followers. They stood in a circle, becoming quiet when he approached.

"What is it now?" he asked.

"We've followed you for days," they said. "It's time you did a real miracle for us."

"What about the cell phones, the vending machine, the kites, the shade? Weren't those miracles?"

A couple came forward, hand in hand. "We want a divorce," they said.

"Lawyers perform divorces," said Carlos. "Not holy men."

"Lawyers cost a lot of money. And they take time. And no one is happy afterward."

He laughed. "So you want me to make you happy too? That is a miracle."

They all nodded, as though he'd said something profound, and waited.

"I can't do that," said Carlos. "It wouldn't be right for a weatherman to take the work of lawyers anyway."

More couples came forward, holding hands and staring at him. "We won't leave you alone until you divorce each and every one of us."

Carlos saw that his time in the desert had come to an end. The storm still buzzed around him, just a tremor in the air, spitting grains of sand in his face. He had been hiding in the desert just as he'd done in his house, and he felt ashamed.

He got into his car and waved goodbye, the people watching him in their Sunday best, still waiting for a miracle. Carlos pulled onto the highway and headed west toward the coast, the storm swelling fat and black in his rear-view mirror. He would fight it where it was strongest.

If anyone had been on the beach during the storm, they would have seen an old Volkswagen with no windows plow off the road and down to the shore, spraying up sand behind it. They would have seen the car drive out onto the waves, bouncing over their uneven hills, and disappear. The storm, howling and peeling back layers of sand in its anger, followed.

Back in the TV station, the meteorologists crowded in front of their computer screens and typed away on their keyboards, watching the storm come back from the desert and swell until it covered the whole of southern California, a ravenous red blob that pushed toward the coast.

For weeks, the storm circled the Pacific. Fishermen off the coast would find it upon them suddenly, waves tilting their ship, and they would pull up their nets. In with their catch would be Carlos, his yellow raincoat hanging in shreds. He fell onto the deck, stepping on fish and spitting up water, and offered to lead them out of the storm. He shouted directions to the captain and kept the ship steady, asking for tins of food and eating with his fingers. When they were almost back to the harbor, he let the storm pull him overboard and vanished to the wind and the waves, calling out to the fishermen, "Tell the weather girl I'm coming back for her."

Carlos dragged the storm up and down the coast, pressing it against the jet stream and wearing it down. When it went one way, he would jerk it the other, breaking up the clouds and slowing its wind. Feeling that he was strong enough one night, he reached up and grabbed the storm in both hands and pulled it down beneath the water. It collapsed into foam and mist. Carlos stood on top of the waves. The white moon shined down on him, black depths hanging below his feet. Carlos, suspended between, knew that he had finally become the weatherman he had always wanted to be.

While Carlos drove back to the TV station, the team of meteorologists tracked him on the Doppler radar. They saw him break away from the coast and move inland, following Interstate 10. "Something's coming," they told the newscasters, though they couldn't say what.

It had been a year since he'd left the TV station. Carlos pulled up and parked in his old spot. The drive up from the coast had been beautiful the whole way. He'd made sure of it. His Volkswagen was studded with barnacles, and seaweed dangled from the hood. The inside of the car was crusted with salt, and dead fish stank from beneath the seats where they'd gotten caught in the springs and had been unable to get free.

He cleaned himself up in the station's restroom, wishing again that he had a razor. He smelled salty and clean, like someone who'd been at the beach a long time.

When he came out, a group of small men in white shirts and khakis held barometers and stood around the door, breathing hard.

"What are you?" one of the meteorologists asked, his voice full of wonder. The instrument in his hand vibrated to be so close to the weatherman. Upstairs, Carlos could feel the weather girl walking to her office as lightly as a cloud.

Carlos looked at himself in ragged raincoat, his skin dark from the desert, beard touching his chest. He smiled. "I am what you can only name."

He found the weather girl in her office. She was as beautiful as ever, and even now, even after everything that he had been through, Carlos's heart still ached for her.

"You beat the storm," she said. "You're a real weatherman."

Carlos nodded.

She took his hands in hers, Carlos feeling how cool and clean her fingertips were on his palms. "Will you promise to stay here?" she asked him. "Until another weatherman comes to take your place?"

He thought of sharing the office with her, the two of them doing the weather together, raising and dropping storms all over the state. He could say nothing but yes.

"Thank you." The weather girl raised her arms and a gust of wind came in through the window, lifting her into the air. "Finally I can go."

And just like that, she tumbled up onto the wind and was gone. Carlos watched her drift away into the sky and float north, bobbing like a balloon, the sun bright on her hair. The weatherman looked around the office and knew that, once again, he was alone. He picked up the office phone and called his old roommates, telling them that he was a weatherman now and that he was coming home.

The meteorologists crept upstairs, small and rat-like. They looked out the window at the weather girl disappearing on the horizon, then at Carlos sitting down heavily in her old chair.

"What's going to happen now?" they asked.

"Now," said Carlos, looking around the small office that already felt like his. "Now it will rain."

CHIMES

A FAMINE OF MUSIC

The Inventor of Ears

From the door of the inventor's apartment, a man with small satellites bolted to the sides of his head ran out into the night. His head low, he stumbled under streetlights and went downtown, homing in on the grind of traffic and noise of the bars. Back inside, the beautiful inventor started work on another.

Her apartment walls were covered in medical posters stolen from doctors' offices: cross-sections of the inner ear, promotional diagrams of a cochlear implant, ads for hearing aids. Milk-boxes full of components she'd bought wholesale filled most of her living room, aluminum disks and stiff wires piling over the sides, and one box of sixty-six hundred white earbuds she'd bought off of eBay. She would not leave feedback until she had a chance to count them. Under her bed, the neck of a guitar stuck out, covered in dust. A trumpet and a snare drum lay in the darkness beside it.

The inventor stood over a woman on her kitchen counter, mounting the ear-assemblies and attaching them to bone. The inventor's hair—black and thick like smoke—brushed the face of her patient as she worked. For months, she had used dating websites to bring people to her apartment, hundreds a week. She knew there was nothing wrong with using her beauty for science.

When she finished attaching the woman's new ears, she helped her sit up on the countertop. The inventor looked her in the eyes and said, "Tell me what this sounds like." The inventor kicked the wall, yelled at the ceiling, changed the TV to a fishing channel and turned the volume all the way up.

The sound went into the satellites covering the woman's ears, vibrated across guitar strings and trumpet valves hidden inside. "Everything is music," the woman said.

"Go and tell others." She pushed the woman into the street, a symphonic night of traffic, sirens, and bar-talk. The inventor cleaned her counter, smoothed her dress, and prepared for the next one.

The Alley Where Music Lived

There was an alley where music lived, and everyone came to see it. But the last few weeks, the musicians had seen the people change. The concert-goers had heavy satellites covering their ears, the metal disks scraping against each other like deer antlers. They each had long strands of black hair lying across their shoulders.

The musicians played anyway. They played burning, low scotch on their saxophones. They played vodka on their trumpets, long and slow and sad. The people cheered and shouted.

The musicians took a break and checked their instruments, a noisy clearing of throats in mics and popping of strings. They shook blots of saliva out of their trumpets. The people cheered louder. The band members shrugged and picked up their instruments again. In her apartment, the lovely inventor waited for them to come.

One of the musicians took the mic. "We like irony too," he said, "but back to business now." The band pulled out everything they had. The steel guitarists laid down some bourbon on the crowd, while a woman on bongos beat out tequila. A man with two tambourines took his shirt off and threw it, jingling Jagermeister with both hands.

The crowd kept cheering, but some wandered over to a department store, bobbing their heads to the TV displays blaring in the windows. "Something is wrong," said the man with two tambourines. The band stopped playing and grabbed some people from the crowd. They held the fans by their metal ears. "Who did this?" they asked.

It took the crowd a moment to realize the musicians weren't still singing. They told them about the lovely inventor, blushing a little and touching the sides of their heads. The musicians slung their instruments over their backs and deployed in taxis to the inventor's apartment. The concert-goers stayed in the alley, listening.

The Whores Who Drank the Seas

Away from the alley of music, seven brothers stood on a cliff overlooking the ocean to hear the waves dying on the rocks. They'd been doing this for years. They all had new ears that night, each feeling jealous that his brothers, too, had seen the lovely inventor. They stood under a small piece of moon and listened, and nothing was right.

In their new ears, the waves sounded like birds chirping. The seven brothers left. They took a limousine slowly through the city, windows down and satellite ears straining to hear where the sound of the waves had gone. They heard sirens that sounded like folk songs, murders that sounded like cell phones. They kept driving.

As they drifted down the street, a whore approached the car and called out to them. The brothers yelled for the driver to stop and they pulled her inside. "Money," she said, and they gave it to her. "What do you want me to do?" They pressed in close to her on the wide leather seat and angled their large ears. "Speak," they said, "and don't stop until morning." The whore spoke until she lost her voice, but others had crowded around the limo and gotten in, pushing against the doors like waves. They spoke in saltwater, like tears. The brothers paid and paid and paid.

The Inventor's Irreparable Heart

The musicians crowded into the inventor's apartment. They wanted to be angry with her, but she smiled and it was difficult. She took their hands and they stuttered.

Someone finally spoke. "You killed music."

The inventor shook her lovely head. "Music is alive everywhere." She held out her hand for one of the guitars, and a woman gave it to her. The inventor started to play. Her hands yanked the strings, and it was an ugly sound. The musicians heard beer steins shattering. They asked her to stop.

"None of you would teach me," she said.

"You are very lovely," they told her, "but we can't teach you." They took the guitar from her hands.

"No one will listen to you anymore."

The musicians wept. The inventor did too. None of them were satisfied with this.

"What if you give us ears to hear like they do?" a woman asked.

The inventor looked at her carefully. "You will have to give me your instruments."

The musicians talked about it and didn't know what else to do. They handed the inventor their finger-marked drums, their scuffed guitars, their scratched trumpets—all the things they loved most in the world. The inventor broke the instruments over her counter and dug out the parts she needed with a lovely finger. She lay the musicians on the counter one at a time and attached the ear-assemblies. Her black hair swept over their faces as she worked. They watched her eyes and felt her hands stroking their heads. They couldn't help but forgive her.

When she was done, the inventor pushed them out one by one and locked her door afterward. The musicians got separated and wandered alone in and out of alleys. One of them found a clarinet sticking out of a trash bag and raised it to his lips. Everything he did sounded the same, and he threw the instrument at a wall, yelling curses at the inventor who'd tricked them. The others heard and ran to him, thinking it was singing.

The Famine of Music

No one was interested in radio stations or music stores anymore. These buildings were shoved farther and farther to the edges of the city. Finally, they picked up their concrete shells and crawled away for good, leaving empty lots behind them.

It was a new world of sound, and the people felt responsible for it. They spread themselves thin over the city so that no sound would be wasted. Wherever a roach crawled, a bus braked, or a newspaper blew over the road, at least one pair of satellite ears was there to hear its music. The people watched each other from the opposite ends of streets and wished they could be together.

Then a rainstorm came, a gray blanket falling over them. There was sound everywhere, lovely and too much of it to be heard. People ran down the sidewalks trying to hear it all, but couldn't. They found each other in the dark, wet streets, resting their heavy heads together and sharing their regret. Sad lovers went back to their apartments that night, rain hammering their windows, and remembered each other's bodies. There would be children.

The Guitars on their Backs

Years later, a troop of mariachis broke down in the middle of nowhere. They got out and looked around, saw tall buildings in the distance, the silhouettes shaggy with ivy. Knowing they had no choice, the mariachis slung their guitars over their backs, put on their wide hats and hard boots, and went into the city to find help.

They walked down cracked roads webbed with grass. Since the radio stations left years ago, cars had quit coming here, pulled back by the arms of radio. The mariachis came like heroes out of the trees and into the center of town. There were children spaced evenly down the streets, their small ears pressed against the road or the sides of buildings. Some cupped their hands to hear better and listened to the wind. None of them understood.

Some of the kids saw the mariachis and waved to them. They'd never seen anything like this before, and called for the tall men in their black uniforms to come closer so they could see.

The men smiled at each other and pulled their guitars off their backs. Mariachis did not come when called. They started playing fast, something sandy and rough, something that stuck in the throat, a sound the kids had never heard and weren't old enough for. Children ran from every part of the city. The mariachis pulled themselves onto an old stage in an alley where music had once lived, and they played, sweeping out their hats to collect money between songs. The kids paid and paid and paid. They called their parents to come bring them money. The parents came, heads bent with the weight of their ears. Seeing the instruments made them feel like they'd lost something, but they couldn't remember what.

When the mariachis had collected a lot of money, they bowed and started to walk away. They were stopped by the inventor, a little older now, but still lovely. They plucked their strings at each other when they saw her and grinned like dogs.

"I'm sorry," she told them. "I did an awful thing."

The mariachis conferred. They said they would forgive her if she gave each of them a kiss. They swept the wide hats from their heads and stared at her, each one wanting the others to die and burning for this woman. The children gathered around and hoped for something to happen.

The inventor went to the first man. She put her arms around his neck, leaned over his shoulder, and kissed the neck of the guitar sticking up from his back. The six strings cut into her lips she kissed the instrument so hard. Her hair fell over the mariachi's shoulder, piling on the back of his neck, and that's when he knew that she owned him. She went to each man and did the same.

The mariachis tried to speak, but couldn't. They blushed and stuttered their thanks. They lay their guitars at her feet and told her that she didn't need to apologize to anyone.

The inventor gave their guitars to the children, keeping one for herself. She turned it over in her hands, looking at how it was put together. "There will be more of these," she told them. "I'll make new ones tonight and bring them tomorrow. Things will be better from now on."

The Strangely Contented Elderly

Satellite signals from space broke apart the vines and sent radio back into the city. The roads opened again. Everyone got older, and the people put their strange parents away.

In a nursing home built on a cliff over the sea, a ward of elderly with satellite ears sat on couches and in wheelchairs. They shot marbles at each other and slid checkers over paper boards, inclining their heads and thrilling in the sounds. The nurses believed they were the happiest of people.

In another room, the old musicians sat in a circle. They had broken their ears off a long time ago, bolts and wires sticking out of the sides of their heads, and they were quite deaf. One at a time, each musician placed a guitar in his lap, and the others reached out to touch it. The musician plucked his way through songs, letting the vibrations in his fingers tell him he was doing it right. The others nodded their heads, tasting the wine in it. They grinned at what nurses didn't know.

Upstairs, a family of seven brothers and seven whores sat in front of the windows looking out on the sea. The whores spoke day and night, their throats hard from years of talking. The brothers watched the waves and patted their wives' hands, listening.

Down in the lobby, an old woman with long hair, still the loveliest woman anyone knew, sat plucking noise from a guitar. Her satellite ears pushed her hair out in two round bumps on the sides of her head. The nurses didn't understand why she liked the sound. They asked her, but she would only say that she didn't need to apologize for anything. The nurses shrugged and believed this was true.

THE BUTCHER'S CHIMES

YOU'VE HEARD STORIES of the old woman before, the one who lived deep in the woods outside of town. Two oak trees squeezed the sides of her house, and no one could tear the ivy off without taking the siding with it. She had a utility pole in the yard and power coming in, serving the few electrical sockets that still worked. Homemade wind chimes dripped from the sagging eaves of the house, strung in messy clumps off through the trees. Metal pipe, skinned sticks, strips of hard plastic, glass beads, and pieces of tin were tied into arrays with fishing line and wire. On a windy day, the chimes made the whole forest mutter.

She had inherited nine children from her daughter who had died, and the nine kids took turns hurting her: one was always sick, one was always breaking a window or a dish, and one was always causing problems at the school. As soon as she took care of one child, one of the other nine would start. She did their laundry, washed dishes, cooked for them, soldered their broken toys, and kept fixing things until metal and wood and green circuit boards grew so thin, they fell apart in her old hands. The old woman lived in her shoes, even slept in them, always on her feet.

It was the middle of summer, and she lined up her nine kids—the eldest boy watching the youngest girl, the twins standing together, the two middle boys, the three middle girls—and took them all to the landfill. They spread out in the shadows of bulldozers and the ruins of cars, turning over soggy black bags and tearing open discarded appliances. Some things the old woman knew how to fix, and they would take home vacuums, blenders, hammers without handles. Anything she couldn't fix, she lopped the electrical cords off, laying the cut cords over her arm like tails, and gave them to her children to burn and then rake the copper out of the sizzling tar of insulation. After they had loaded all this into stolen shopping carts, they combed over the mounds of junk for things that the old woman could use to make wind chimes and sell on the roadside.

The old woman thought the chimes were beautiful, complex and gleaming and sharp. When she pulled the fishing line and wire through her teeth to make it straight, the strings twitched like insects. Anything she tied with them would come alive. She dreamed of seeing her chimes over every door, on every tree, but she hadn't been able to sell very many.

After they got back from the landfill, the old woman took the three middle girls with her to sell chimes. The girls were in their early teens, slim with long black hair and dark skin. The old woman stood them by the road in their summer clothes, leaning back against a wobbly card table set up on the shoulder and piled with chimes. She told the girls to wave to men who passed in their cars. The men would stop.

They'd been standing there for around four hours when a man in a brown car came by and pulled over. He wore a black hat and his hands were covered in dried blood. The old woman and her daughters could see a mound of packages wrapped in damp white paper in his backseat.

The girls smiled and told him they liked his hat, as they were supposed to. They touched the brim.

"Did you have an accident?" the old woman asked.

"No," said the man. "The meat fair's come again. This year, the Cleaver has six acres of butchers' booths."

She untangled one of the chimes from the pile. "Brown is the color for a man who likes meat. This is handmade with root beer glass. See what it does to the light? Hear that sound?"

The man looked at several more chimes, talking to the girls and asking which they liked best. Finally, he took the root beer chime, dumped it into his passenger seat, and left. He gave them fifteen dollars for it, all they made that day. Soon, she would have to do something to keep all her children fed.

The old woman and the girls packed their things and walked back home, rolling the card table on its side through the woods. They came to the house, the three middle girls hooking the unsold chimes back under the eaves with the others. She spent the rest of the afternoon working on an old deep freeze, unable to think of anything but the swollen packages in the back of the man's car. She finally got the freezer to hum back to life. Then it was late, so she put all her children to bed and went into the kitchen to sort the piles of pipe and glass. She unballed the tangled wire and fishing line and pulled it through her teeth until it was straight. They lay in clean rows on the table, wagging like tails and eager to move chimes. The freezer buzzed from the other room while she worked.

She got her children up early the next morning. "Put Ziplock bags in your pockets," she told them. "Line the insides of your clothes with plastic wrap and newspaper. We're going to the meat fair." They walked under the trees in the dim light, the chimes clattering above their heads.

The old woman, wearing a wide straw hat, herded her children inside the gates. There were hundreds of people, big fabric tents everywhere, and every kind of meat. There were sides of cow swaying from chains, plucked and unplucked birds hanging by their feet, ice bins stuffed with small, fatted rodents. Dorsal fins were stacked like chips on wire stringers, swimming pools stank with shellfish, and frozen frogs filled boxes. People dodged yellow columns of flypaper hanging from tent edges, vibrating with wing and leg and eye. Kids went to booths where they tried to guess their weight in chicken hearts or threw darts at inflated animal bladders. Nothing was labeled, but the butchers assured everyone that there was no kind of meat they didn't have.

The Cleaver was somehow everywhere at once. He was a huge man, big-bellied and shining with sweat. His white shirt curled at the bottom, sliding up his stomach and sides. He wore rough leather gloves and delicate glasses. He spun the animals hanging overhead and lopped off slices of them with his knife, dropping the crescent-shaped hacks into wads of white butcher paper and filling his pockets with the meat-eaters' money. The hot dog vendors and fry pits buzzed with people, but could not move the Cleaver. He ate only vegetables himself. Had the old woman's eyes been better, she would have seen that the Cleaver was a man who believed in punishment.

She whispered for her kids to be careful and to run if anyone caught them. The nine children spread out over the fair and mixed with the crowds of people waving off flies and haggling over meat. Their small hands stole into bowls of livers, picked drumsticks from lines, pushed into ice-bins packed with cuts of steak. They fished out pickled sow-ears from jars and peeled off marbled strips of beef, filling their pockets and clothes with the chilled, spongy hunks of flesh. One of the twins had brought a backpack and, stopping for a moment, was able to slip it over a grinning hog's head. He could feel the snout pushing into his back with every step.

Everywhere they went, the Cleaver saw them and ran his thumb over the blade of his knife while counting what they took. He saw their soggy pants' pockets bulging, the sticky tips of their fingers. He imagined them chewing it raw in the parking lot, cooking up stinking vats in their oven at home, rolling charred bits of it between their teeth, and this disgusted him. He would make sure that they left with no more than they had come.

They left the fair as soon as the sky began to dim, the old woman leading her children in a long line on the shoulder, car-lights sweeping back and forth across them in the dark. After a while, they turned into the forest, pushing their way through the dark brush and avoiding the black columns of the trees, until finally they saw the blue glow of their yard ahead. Once they were all back under the lights of their house, their take of meat tossed in the freezer, the old woman saw that there were only eight children. One of the twins, the girl, was missing. She flexed her feet in her old shoes, took the oldest boy and three middle girls with her, and went out with flashlights to find the lost twin.

While they were gone, the other children went through the freezer to see what everyone had gotten. "We'll have bacon first," the youngest girl said.

"That isn't bacon," said one of the middle boys.

"It's a lot like it, though. We could call it bacon."

They took everything out of the freezer, pushed the old woman's chime parts out of the way, and put all the meat on the table where they could see it: a small hog's head, a whole turkey, a leg of deer, a side of ribs, a couple of drumsticks, and lots of smaller pieces they couldn't identify. The twin said it looked like a person piled up the way it was, and the others agreed. They grabbed some of the strings that the old woman had straightened and cut, the lines trembling with life in their hands. Then they found a needle and started stitching the clumps of meat together. They picked it up and set it in a chair where they could look at what they'd done.

"We'll call you pigboy," the lonely twin said. He hugged it, making his shirt sticky and damp. "Until my sister gets back, you can be my twin."

The pigboy cocked his head at the twin and opened his jaw. "You won't get her back," he said. "Not if the Cleaver has her."

"You don't know that," said the twin, "You're made of meat!"

"So are you!" said the pigboy. He jumped out of the chair and started circling the kitchen, dragging his bony knobs over the floor, rooting through the cabinets under the sink, butting against the table, and enjoying his new life. The children followed him around the house and cleaned up after him, eventually cornering the pigboy in the living room.

"We're going to be in trouble," the girl said.

"Will I be in trouble?" asked the pigboy.

"You most of all," said the twin.

§

The old woman, the three middle girls, and the oldest boy had been out walking for hours and hours. They went all the way down the dark road back to the fair gates, chained shut and rattling in the wind. The old woman leaned on the fence and listened to the fair: the hum of refrigeration units, the creak of the fences and snap of the tent fabric, the tumble of crushed beer cans rolling around on the gravel, even the slick hiss of ice cubes melting in the heavy shadows under tables. She shuddered. It all had a bad sound to her.

They went back down the road, calling out on the roadsides and through the low places of the forest for the twin they had lost, but they couldn't find her. The old woman took her kids under the hard, clean lights of a gas station and left them clustered around a broken fuel pump while she went inside to borrow the phone. She watched them through the window, dark and dirty as rats, heads lifting at the strange smell of gasoline. They all held hands and flinched from the cars pulling in and out. The old woman called the police and told them about her missing daughter.

When the old woman, the eldest boy, and the three middle girls came through the door of the house, it was well past midnight. They stopped in the living room, seeing the pigboy sitting in a chair with its mismatched arms folded over its turkey stomach, the youngest girl, two middle boys, and the lonely twin sitting on the floor around it. The pigboy said good evening to the old woman. The other children had told it that its chances would be better if it was polite.

The old woman and the older group of children sat down on the floor too. She massaged the bottoms of her feet through the thin soles of her shoes. "Tell me everything you know about the Cleaver," she said.

The pigboy's nose started to bleed slowly, two thin lines that trickled down his snout and fell to his chest. He lapped at the blood with a stunted tongue, smearing it. "He rips, and he cuts, and he cleaves. That's all a Cleaver is. I can tell you about old women too."

The old woman narrowed her eyes at him. "We're talking about Cleavers. If we brought you back, would he return my daughter?"

The pigboy shook his head. "Cleavers don't give. They know only buying and selling."

The old woman got up and went into the kitchen. She came back with a loaf of bread and smeared the slices with lard, handing them out to her children and telling them to eat. "There won't be any meat tonight," she said. She put them all to bed, the pigboy shoving himself into the lost twin's pajamas and crawling into the topmost bunk. The other twin lay on the bed beneath it, crying for his lost sister and cradling a pillow. The old woman lay down in bed, her shoes sticking out from underneath her blanket and heavy on her feet. She thought of the children she had lost and covered her face with her hands.

The lonely twin lay in his bed thinking about what his lost sister might have eaten for dinner that night. If she was still inside the meat fair, maybe she had eaten hot dogs and fried chicken legs, or things they'd never even heard of. He wondered if he was a bad twin for making the pigboy and letting him wear his sister's pajamas. He crept out of bed and was on his way out the door when he heard a scraping on the floor behind him. The pigboy stood in the hallway, a blanket wrapped around his shoulders and head.

The twin held up a finger for him to be quiet. The pigboy headed out the door with him, through the clouds of dipping white moths under the blue light and into the black growth of the trees.

"What are we doing?" the pigboy asked.

"We're going to sneak inside the fair and find out what happened to my sister before the Cleaver wakes up."

The two of them ran to the road and jogged the few miles back to the fair. They climbed over the gate and headed between the tents, the pigboy leading the way to the trailers where the Cleaver kept everything that was important to him.

The refrigeration units on the backs of the trailers filled the fairground with a metallic droning. They tried three different ones before they found one that was unlocked. Inside, the metal floor was frozen over and clumps of bloody ice drizzled down the walls. There was a dim light in the top of the trailer, shining on sides of beef, stacks of chickens and turkeys in bins, and tubs with a mix of everything from chicken necks to cat bellies to crab legs. Lying on top, gleaming red under the light, was a long, thin section of skinned muscle and bone.

"That's an arm," said the twin.

"That's *something's* arm," said the pigboy.

"There's no hand or skin, but you can tell what it is. He carved her up, just like you said."

"He carves things. That's what a Cleaver does."

Shoving his fist into his mouth so as not to cry, the twin grabbed the arm and ran out of the trailer, the pigboy chasing after. The twin was almost back to the gate when the Cleaver grabbed him by the shoulder, shoved him inside a concession trailer, and shut the door behind them. The Cleaver's body took up all the space in the tiny room. No matter how he stood, the twin felt the Cleaver's bulk pushing against him.

The twin shook the arm at him. "This is my sister," he said.

"Call it whatever you want. You'll pay meat for meat," the Cleaver said.

The pigboy had made it back to the fence and scrambled over. He lay in a ditch by the road, his ears pricked up, listening to the sounds from inside the fair.

The sun had just come up when the old woman woke to the lonely twin standing over her, his eyes red and swollen, his shirt damp. His left arm ended in a butcher-paper bandage just below the shoulder. "I found her arm and tried to take it," he said. "So the Cleaver took mine."

She stared at his arm and could only think of chimes, wire and pipe, things she could understand. "Show me what you found," she said.

Going through the living room, all the other kids were up, watching the pigboy bat the skinned limb back and forth over the wooden floor.

"What are you doing?" the old woman asked.

The pigboy picked up the arm and shook it at her. "It's a dog leg," he said. "Aren't dogs fun?"

The twin started crying and all the children talked at once.

"Does this mean our sister is okay?" the youngest girl asked.

But the pigboy wasn't paying attention to anything but the leg. He shoved the end of it into the soft meat of his crotch until it stuck there, then thrust his body so that it would swing back and forth. "Aren't dogs fun?" he said again. He said it over and over, swinging his body so hard that his seams stretched and cut across his flesh.

"Stop it!" the old woman yelled. All nine of them stopped talking at once, the pigboy losing his footing and falling into a heap on the floor.

"Good evening," he said.

The old woman pulled the pigboy into the kitchen and turned on the oven. All morning, the eight children watched her stuff his crevices full of yellow granules for poisoning ants, pour liquid termite killer down his throat, and fill his gut with green, flat discs of rat poison. She shoved him down into a heavy iron pot, the pigboy shaking and his nose bleeding, and poured a half empty jar of applesauce over him. She sent seven of her children, keeping the twin with her, out to collect the small, sour apples that grew wild in the woods, and she smashed those and added them too, the tart smell covering over the poison. She added cinnamon, clouds of it floating in the sunlight through the window. Then she opened the oven door, an exhalation of heat flooding the kitchen.

The pigboy looked around at the faces looming over him, the old woman and the children. "Lots of hands are good for chime-making," the pigboy said, "and the old woman loves her chimes."

"What's he talking about?" asked one of the girls.

The old woman squinted at her, trying to remember which one she was. "Nothing. It doesn't matter. We'll get your sister back."

"One sister is two hands for chime-making." The pigboy said this very seriously.

The children felt the weight of the chimes moving in the forest, creaking on the eaves, the guts of them strewn across all the tables and counters, their glass and strings stretching back for years, as long as they could remember.

"That's enough." The old woman put her shoe on the edge of the pot and shoved him deep into the oven with her foot, slamming the door. "The pigboy is the Cleaver's creature. Don't listen to anything he says." The children dispersed through the house, not talking, while the old woman cleaned up.

A few hours later, she opened it and pulled him out. The applesauce had caramelized over the meat. It filled the house with sweet-smelling smoke. The pigboy's eyes were cooked down to stains and his jaw hung open, his tiny teeth standing up from black gums.

The old woman loaded the pot into a wheelbarrow and told her kids to wait for her at home. She put a sheet over it and wheeled it over tree roots and heaps of leaves, through the forest and back out to the road. She pulled the wheelbarrow onto the shoulder, where the man who had told them about the fair had stopped, and pushed it along the side of the highway.

When she rolled through the fair gates, the smell made people stop and press in close to her. "It smells so good!" they said. "Look at it, sitting up in its own juices, arms out just begging to be eaten. Let us taste."

She smiled and shook her head. "Every bite is for the Cleaver."

The old woman found him cutting rib-bones clean and white and laying them in rows across a table. She thought what excellent chimes they would make, could hear their bony clatter just by looking at them. The Cleaver asked her what she wanted.

The old woman stared at his greasy face, the bloody knife hanging from his belt. "I want my daughter back," she said.

The Cleaver squinted at her, still sliding his knife over bones. "I have as much meat as is mine," he said.

"I brought back everything. I even cooked it, just for you. Take it."

The Cleaver leaned over the wheelbarrow, holding his breath so as not to smell it. He rolled the cooked pigboy into the tent behind them, then came back and fished through his wallet. He handed the old woman a check someone had written him for thirty-five dollars.

"A customer this morning bought her live, whole and uncut. The address is on the check."

"Bought her live?" the old woman asked.

"Yes. Like a lobster." The Cleaver stared at her, wondering why she didn't understand.

The Cleaver watched the old woman run out the gate. He brought people back and showed them the cooked meat in the wheelbarrow, tearing off pieces of it with tongs and dropping it into squares of paper in his hand, pricing it by the handful. They ate it on hot dog buns, in chili bowls, in their hands, the crowd growing and growing. When the Cleaver cut deeper, he saw green and yellow swirls staining the meat, and he knew that something was wrong.

Yelling rose from the middle of the fairgrounds, and sirens flew toward them from every direction. The Cleaver went to see and found yellow lines of vomit on the grass, people lying on the ground. The butchers were swearing in front of their stalls and throwing their tongs at one another, each one blaming the others for selling spoiled meat. Through the gates, health inspectors and police came in with silver badges and wide-brimmed hats. They told the Cleaver that they were shutting it all down. They said that all the meat would have to be thrown out, just to be safe. The Cleaver shut his eyes and cursed the old woman who had ruined him.

The old woman had gone all the way into town, walking as fast as she could in her old shoes. She came to a green, open place with white houses and square lawns. Sprinklers stuttered and wet the sidewalks. SUVs shuddered heavy in and out of driveways, and she shrank from their clean weight. Counting the golden mailbox numbers going toward the address on the check, the old woman came to a yard where two young girls were playing in the sprinklers and laughing.

Had her eyes been better, the old woman would have seen that neither of them was her daughter. She thought she recognized the voice of the lost twin and pushed her way into the shrubs to wait. The girls were jumping through the water and shrieking, the bottoms of their feet flashing pink against the grass. The old woman squinted harder. That one. It had to be that one.

She reached through the bushes with her hard arms and grabbed one of the girls by her shoulders. The old woman dragged her through the bushes, squeezed her tight to her chest, and ran into the shadowy space behind the houses and off the road. The girl tried to scream, but the old woman slapped her mouth. She whispered a little nursery rhyme to the girl, over and over. The girl listened to it with wide eyes the whole way, her body limp with fear.

From the main road, police lights licked the asphalt and sent colors dancing through the trees. The old woman turned for the deep woods away from the sirens, away from the town and the fairground, away from gas stations and sprinklers, and headed back to her house.

It was late at night when she finally got in, and all her children were up waiting. She walked inside and set the girl down on the floor, her eyes swollen. "Your sister is home," the old woman said.

Her other eight kids stared at her, silent.

"It's okay now," the old woman said. She turned to the lonely twin. "The Cleaver paid for what he did to you." The old woman hugged the girl, and she shivered in her bathing suit, not making a sound.

The twin said, "That isn't my sister."

The rest agreed. She had taken the wrong girl.

"You don't know what you're saying. Of course this is your sister."

"You're lying."

"Who said that?" The old woman looked over the rows of bleary faces, the kids getting mixed up in her head with her childhood friends, her own children, her other grandchildren, other kids she'd seen or found.

"The pigboy was right." They spoke as if with one voice. "You only care about making the chimes." They called her a child stealer. They said she was just like the Cleaver. They asked what had happened to their mother, and they blamed the old woman for everything bad in their lives.

The old woman closed her eyes and leaned against the wall. The years came down on her old shoulders all at once, her feet hard and sore in the shoes she lived in. Not knowing what to do, the old woman did what she had always done. She yelled for them to shut up and chased them all over the house, whipping them one after another, even the new girl, until they lay in their beds shaking under the covers. Then the old woman went to lie down herself, but couldn't sleep. She got up and went into the kitchen, the empty freezer humming loudly from the other room. She pushed around the pieces of pipe and branches, untangling the wire and fishing line and pulling it through her teeth until it was straight and alive.

Outside, the chimes rattled along the sides of the house, so numerous they made the eaves groan. She closed her eyes and listened. It was a good sound.

CLEANING THE FLEABOY

THEY FOUND THE FLEABOY on the side of the highway standing over a dead dog. Shirley stopped the car, and her family—Shirley, her husband Bill, daughter Kate, and son Drew—stared at him through the windows of their blue SUV.

The fleaboy was about seven years old and wore an adult-size t-shirt with no shoes or pants. His skin was spotted with bright red flea bites, and a shifting mass of black fleas flowed over his skin like a watery coat of paint.

Shirley saw him beside the dog carcass and knew that he needed someone. "We can help him," she said.

Drew text-messaged his friend, *Things don't look good.*

Kate was reading a book, and their father said nothing.

Shirley turned around to address the car. "We're bringing him home with us." No one moved as Shirley got out, picked up the fleaboy, and tucked him into the backseat. The boy did not speak.

On the drive home, the fleaboy sat cross-legged between Kate and Drew, the teenagers pressed against their doors. They could feel it when the fleas lit on them, the tiny bodies sailing through the air, the tickle when the fleas dropped onto their skin and bulled beneath the crossing hairs of their arms, following veins up toward their necks.

Fleas filled the car. Drew texted, *I think the world is ending.* Kate yelled for their mother to pull over and dump the fleaboy out. "There's the creek," Kate said. "People drop cats off there all the time." The air shimmered with black fleas popping their legs and firing off the gray upholstery, passing one another in flight, gliding through jeans and shirts.

Bill, a man who believed in his things, tried to find a button in the car that would kill fleas. He turned the radio all the way up, turned the air conditioner as cold as it would go, rolled down the windows, and reached past his wife's hand on the steering wheel to engage the lights, turn on the windshield wipers, and spurt cleaning fluid all over the glass. By the time they pulled into the driveway, he was nearly in tears.

The sun was bright, and neighbor kids played tennis with fluorescent rackets in the street outside their house. Shirley pulled the SUV into the garage and killed it. While she took the fleaboy by the hand and led him inside, her family walked into the sun and heat of the yard to beat the lingering fleas out of their clothes. They hit themselves across the chest and limbs while the neighbors grinned. "Pack of jackasses," Bill said. "When it happens to them, they won't think it's so funny. You tell them," Bill told his son, and Drew texted his friends what his father thought of them.

Inside the house, Shirley carried the fleaboy up the stairs. She felt a crawling on her scalp, and she whined in her throat, running for the bathroom. She set him down in the tub, not bothering to take off his t-shirt, and turned on the shower. The fleaboy rolled in his dirty underwear and shirt, the tub turning brown. The surface of the water trembled with a hundred crisscrossing ripples, the fleas kicking to free themselves. They washed up against the rim and crawled up, a rising ring of black.

For the next hour and a half, Shirley scrubbed the fleaboy pink with brushes, washed his oily blond hair, and bathed him in everything she had, from advanced-hair-care-formula-with-curl-protection to blue ocean Suave to Dawn dish liquid. She sent thousands of leggy black specks swirling down the drain, but there were always more.

As Shirley washed him, the fleas reconnoitered her body, learning every line and mole of her. They filled the thick bathroom mat and toilet seat cover. They bounced down the stairs and swam in schools through the carpet.

When Bill and the kids opened the door, fleas catapulted themselves out of the rugs, hairy legs hooking into the fibers of their shirts. Horrified, they went back outside.

Later in the evening, Bill came in and found Shirley mopping the floors furiously, fleas crawling over her face and thrashing on the soapy tiles. The vacuum lay on the floor in the living room, hot to the touch and smelling awful, its dustbin ricocheting with life.

He took her shoulders in his hands and made her look at him, fleas wandering over both of their faces. The fleaboy sat in the middle of the floor, his t-shirt sticking to him. "Honey," Bill said, "There's something wrong with this kid."

Bill and Shirley drove the fleaboy to the hospital. They sat in the waiting room for several hours. Bill held a magazine in his lap and stared down at his shoes, grass stains across the tops of his gray sneakers. Today wasn't supposed to have been like this.

Shirley sat up straight in her chair, French-manicured hands folded in her lap. Everyone who came back from the doctors' rooms had fleas on their clothes. Her stomach felt bad, and she pulled a roll of antacids out of her purse.

A nurse called them back, taking them to a tiny room with the fleaboy sitting up on the examination bed, eating a sucker. The doctor looked at them and shook his head.

"What's wrong?" Shirley asked. "How can we help him?"

"There's no helping him," the doctor said. "It's genetic. He has fleas in his blood."

On the way home, Bill drove the car. He slowed down by the creek, abandoned cats staring at them with yellow eyes from the bushes, little tins of cat food left by someone glinting in the streetlight. "Maybe the boy could be happy here," Bill said.

Shirley smacked her cheek and pinched a flea between her fingers. It left a red blot on her thumb. "No," she said. "He comes home with us."

When they got back, Bill made Drew help him build a doghouse in the garage. Drew texted his friends—*Times are bad*—and handed his father tools. They set the doghouse out in the yard and put the fleaboy inside with an old blanket. Shirley brought him a package of Oreos and two Dr. Peppers.

She stood at the mouth of the doghouse after everyone had gone inside, listening to the fleaboy root around in his blanket and crinkle the package of cookies. He hadn't spoken since they'd found him. He fumbled with the tab on the can of soda, but Shirley had clipped his fingernails too short and he couldn't get it. She listened to his blunt fingers tap against the top of the can, and her heart broke.

"Scoot over," she said.

Shirley crawled inside the doghouse, fleas cascading to her from every wall and making her shiver. She helped him open the can, wrapped the blanket around them both, and held the boy close to her. He buried his flea-covered head in her neck. By morning, she had made up her mind.

She brought the fleaboy inside as her family was having breakfast. They dipped their spoons into cold bowls of cereal, socks swinging under their chairs. Shirley's hair was stiff and her clothes were badly wrinkled, dirt on her knees. She held the fleaboy's hand, and her face was serious. They'd never seen her like this before.

"We're not keeping him out in the yard like a dog. And we're not dropping him off at the creek like a cat. Our lives are just going to be different now."

Bill stared down at his cereal, the flakes softening in the milk, and clinked his spoon against the side of his bowl. "I like the way things are," he said.

Shirley squeezed his shoulder. "I'm sorry. From now on, we all have fleas."

§

Shirley stopped trying to keep the house clean, knowing it would do no good, and gave up on being able to kill the fleas crawling over her. Vermin bedded down in the carpets and assailed the legs of anyone walking through the living room. Kate and Drew started wearing shorts inside so that they could pick the fleas off their legs. Bill mixed cheap dish liquid and water in spray bottles and kept them around the house to squirt his legs and arms or spray down the carpet when the fleas got bad. Their house smelled like Dawn.

The fleaboy was more active now. He played in the dirt in the backyard or watched television with the rest of them. Sometimes he spoke, telling them about things he'd seen that made him think of fleas: stars, dandelion seeds, gravel, even people if you were far enough away. He slept in the laundry room, on a heap of whatever hadn't been washed that day, burying his face in Shirley's dirty jeans and shirts.

Bill had friends over from work eventually, and they noticed things. The house more rundown than ever, the kids looking less healthy, the ugly red welts, the way Shirley's nails were bitten down, her hair frizzy and matted. They went back to their homes and talked. Kate and Drew told their friends from school, and the story of the fleaboy moved from person to person, spreading across the whole town. The clerks at the grocery store watched Shirley pick out frozen pizzas in sweatpants, one hand always clawing at her skin, a sleepy smile on her face. They thought of how Shirley had been before, and of the blond boy in the oversized shirt they had seen doing cartwheels in the grass behind the house.

One morning the doorbell rang, and when Shirley answered it, the entire town stood on her front lawn. They'd come in SUVs and cars, on motorcycles and in trucks. A line of bikes lay against the chain-link fence. People filled her yard all the way out to the road and down the street, people as thick as fleas, as far as she could see. They wore their best clothes, hair wet with gel and shirts pressed and buttoned to the collar.

The mayor spoke first: "We need to talk to you about the fleaboy."

Hearing his name, the boy ran to the door to see who was there, and Shirley picked him up. Bill and his kids looked on the crowd from an upstairs window, feeling its breath shake the glass. "They'll make her get rid of him," Bill told his kids, "and things will be like they were."

They said they were glad, not sure if they meant it anymore. Bill remembered the boy diving into the shallow swimming pool behind the house, how he'd watched and smoked cigarettes, skimming the fleas off the water with a net and flicking their chlorinated bodies into the yard. "People just don't live this way," he said, though he didn't know very much about people or how they lived.

At the doorway, Shirley held the boy and looked at them, the ocean of faces that she knew. "What do you have to say to us?"

The school principal spoke first: "Even a fleaboy should go to school," she said. Then the coach: "And after school, he should go to karate practice." More and more people from the town chimed in: "After that, the grocery store to pick out his favorite flavor of Pop-Tarts. On Sundays, to the ice cream shop to have a banana split, like the other kids do." Shirley's neighbors nodded. They said, "We should have a chance to be as good as you."

Shirley didn't know what to say. She walked out to the crowd and gave the fleaboy over to the town. In the weeks following, he started school and played sports. He got his hair cut, helped Bill pick out cigars, and rode the bus to school. The fleas poured off his body and got on all the kids. The kids brought them home and gave them to their parents. The parents gave them to their dogs. The fleas covered the whole town, until it smelled like soap and pesticide, and the grass grew thick in the yards, and people stopped in the grocery store to talk about hairspray or furniture polish or air freshener that also killed fleas. Everything became run-down, the roads cracked and houses unpainted, all the cars unwashed. Nothing was like it had been. Anyone driving through wouldn't have stopped. They would have been able to tell at once that something was very different here.

IN A CITY

IN A CITY OF RAIN and brick, neon haze and cigarette smoke, the gentlemen came every Thursday, crawling from the wet into a small theater to hear three lovely singers: a soprano, an alto, and a tenor. The gentlemen shook off their damp coats and pressed against each other in the entryway. They were small and pale in coal-black suits with hats and canes. They packed hip to hip in the dark wooden seats of the theater, and they waited.

A light bloomed on the black wood stage. The singers walked out and faced the mass of cricket-like gentlemen twitching in the seats of the auditorium. The tenor, tall and plump, wore a black gown with rhinestones across her mountainous breasts. The alto, a girl with coffee-colored hair and eyes, wore a plain black dress. The soprano, so tiny as to be only diaphanous blond hair and long-fingered hands, wore a gown the color of cream. They lifted their faces and began.

The tenor's voice was low, and it moved through the gathered gentlemen like the vibrations of subway lines passing below their feet. The alto's song pushed through the rows like a crowd of people, brushing against the gentlemen and moving them around in their seats. The sound went all the way to a young boy in the balcony who wrapped his arms around himself to feel the lovely alto so near. But the other gentlemen watched the soprano. She wailed, rolling out smokestack arias, her voice thick like smog, sweeping down the gentlemen's throats and saturating their clothes until they even stank of her voice. They crouched low behind their seat-backs, hard shoes trembling against the floor and mouths working open and shut.

After the performance, the three bowed and left the stage. The gentlemen thumped their canes and waved their hats. They rushed to meet the ladies beside the stage door, offering their cold hands and sweeping the singers up in sooty hugs. Always the soprano was mobbed, the gentlemen clicking their tongues rudely at each other as they fought for the touch of her hand. The tenor had her select group who held themselves above the rest and who, a few minutes after the show was over, pulled her off into the dark pubs of the city to buy her Scotch and kiss her heavy knuckled hands. But the alto had no one. It was her job to fill the space and create the body of the piece, not to stand out.

The boy watched her from the balcony and wanted to go to her, but she was too beautiful for him to speak to. And so the gentlemen marched by the alto, speaking softly and tipping their hats, but did no more than was their obligation. It went on like this for years.

One Thursday, the soprano and the tenor came into the theater, and the alto was not there. They paced and swore, leaving the gentlemen squirming in their seats for an hour, but she never came. Hand in hand, the soprano and the tenor took the stage without her and began to sing. But the heavy quiet of the room, so used to being pushed away by three voices, fell heavily on the singers and swallowed up their song so that the gentlemen could hear nothing, only watched them swaying on the stage in silence. The gentlemen jabbered to each other, wiped their brows nervously, and were afraid.

The boy flailed his cane and pushed his way through the crawling rows until he reached the stage. Looking up into the red eyes of the soprano and tenor, their wide empty mouths, he wondered if he'd lost his chance forever.

After the performance, the gentlemen shook their heads and rushed back into the rain, abandoning the singers. The soprano went alone to the street and stood in the cold, hair and hands limp with water, waiting for someone to call her a cab. The tenor wandered, looking for her pub, but all the glowing signs seemed the same. The next day, the soprano and tenor met, locked the main door of the theater, and did not perform again.

That summer, the boy came squinting down a gravel road into a whitewashed town on the grass. The people there took slow steps. Their shirts were loose and white, their faces full of heat and wind. They had never seen a city. The boy's jacket was sun-grayed, his cane broken, and his shoes thin as cloth at the soles. He hugged the buildings' shadows and crept into the back of a little church. He slept through the service until the very end when the choir rose and a gap-toothed piano started playing. The alto's back was to him, leading a group of young tenors and sopranos. There was not an alto in her choir. She directed the country girls, singing the first few notes, and sound swelled in the room until lines ran in the wallpaper and the sides of the church bowed out. Afterward, people in starched shirts and obscene boots clapped her on the back and grinned whitely, made suggestions for what songs they wanted to hear next time. The boy could not abide it.

Holding the sides of the pews, he scurried to the front and fell down at the hem of the surprised alto. She recognized him as one of the gentlemen, looking threadbare and ill so far from the city of rain and brick.

Shaking, he took her hand. "I've come miles and miles under the gentleman-killing sun. Checked every whitewashed church in the country. And now, I've found you again." He could see his reflection in the glassy curve of her coffee-colored eyes.

The people smiled at each other, not liking the scent of him.

The alto held her hand to her throat and looked down at the boy. She remembered him from the theater, how he'd always sat far in the back where her voice rippled over his head and stirred his hair. In his skin, she could feel the city—wet bricks shifting under her feet, bar signs hovering in the dark, air filled with iron and exhaust on her tongue—and she missed it.

"I could never come back," she told him. "Not after everything."

The boy threw himself around her legs, before he could consider what was proper. "It won't be the same," he told her. "The gentlemen need you. I promise that you'll never feel unloved again."

They sat in the shade behind the church and talked for hours. The alto stroked his hair, felt his eyes and body angled toward her, all of him focused on the notes of her voice alone. She multiplied him in her mind, imagining a theater full of such boys, all there for her song. She knew that she could not stay at the church now.

The white-shirted men kicked the grass and knew that they had lost her. They gave the alto and the boy their blessing, then watched them disappear down the road to the city. Turning back to their church, they found the choir of tenors and sopranos looking sad in their pews, and they wondered where they would ever find another alto.

The alto and the boy got to the theater on a Thursday, but it was closed. The black-coated gentlemen were wandering through the rain and hissing at each other, shaking soggy newspapers under streetlights. They could only remember what Thursdays had been.

The alto led the boy through a side-door into the lightless theater, faded posters peeling from the walls. They found the tenor lying on the stage on heaps of musty-smelling blankets.

The tenor said, "I've waited months for you to come back." The low boom of her voice pushed away the motes of dust that hung in the air.

"I'm sorry for everything," the alto said. "Can you take me to the soprano?"

Dress askew, the tenor led them into the rain. The smoke, wet, and lights of the city were pulling the heat out of the boy's skin. He stood a little straighter. His clothes thickened and mended in the city air. They found the soprano at a music school downtown. She stood at a podium directing a vast auditorium of cream-gowned, young sopranos. From her place on the stage, she turned and looked down at the alto, her face unforgiving.

The alto asked, "What would it take for you to come back?"

The soprano looked at her with hate, then at the young gentleman standing in her shadow.

"Everything," the soprano said.

"Agreed." The alto pushed the shaking boy toward the soprano. She thought of the gentlemen he'd told her about, her imagined theater of boys just like him, all the people who needed her. She could give up one boy.

In a city of rain and brick, neon haze and cigarette smoke, the gentlemen came crawling in from the wet to hear three lovely singers: a soprano, an alto, and a tenor. After the performance, they rushed to meet the ladies at the stage door. Always the soprano was mobbed. The boy stood quietly at her side to hold the roses brought for her and to attend to anything she might want. The tenor had her select group who pulled her off into the dark pubs of the city. But it was the alto's job to create the body of the piece, not to stand out. And so the gentlemen marched by her, tipping their hats, but doing no more than was their obligation.

Afterward, the alto went alone up to the loft above the theater and slept. When it was almost morning, the young gentleman pushed open the loft door and lay down beside her. His trembling coat was still thick with the soprano's voice. The alto stroked his back while he said he was sorry over and over and told her that her voice was all he wanted. The alto did not speak. She hummed, the sound pushing the high ringing out of the boy's head.

It went on like this for years.

THE LOST LOVES OF DANNY LOWE

ALL THE LOST LOVES of Danny Lowe, his lifetime of lonely nights, began that evening at the barn party. Thunder was breaking the sky in half, and the boys ran out of the wet and under the eaves of the barn: Danny, his three older cousins, and his uncle. Danny pressed back into the barn wall, breathing quick and listening to that good rain-sound rattling on the tin-top. The four of them, grinning and ready to go in, all looked down when they saw his uncle watching them. They waited, Danny staring at his uncle's arms crawling with white welder scars and rain-wet. His uncle opened his jaw, told them they'd best behave or he'd put a goddamn hurt on them, by god. This was his boss's party, and they'd better not fuck anything up. He said they was all sorry shits anyways, and they was lucky to get to come.

They said, yessir, and hung their shaggy heads. Danny too.

Nobody needs railcars like they used to, his uncle said, and the boss knows it.

The boys all nodded solemn, knowing it wasn't good, but not what it meant all the way.

His uncle opened the door, and they walked into the light and noise. It was hot and yellow inside and stunk like kerosene. A lot of people Danny didn't know lay around on hay bales and oil-stained benches. In the middle was the wreck of an old railcar, windows spewing smoke from the fish fryer inside, and more smoke from all the men with their cob-pipes and cigars. Bottles clapped against each other, beer sloshing the floor. The far back wall was all hay piled up, gapped with the bales taken and scattered around to catch whiskey and fish vomit. Fiddle players squealed back and forth at each other across the room over the whirling heads of the party folk. Even inside, Danny could hear drumming on the tin overhead, thunderstorm belly-down on them.

His uncle and cousins fell into the people and was gone, and Danny stayed by the door just looking, when he saw a girl wandering around. She was something younger than him, messy hair piling on her cheeks and back, barefoot in the hay. Boss squeezed her shoulder when she walked by—she was his—and all the grown people started talking to her then. She ducked her head from it, put her hands together like a preacher, grinning and shy and walking away like that. Danny lost her then.

He stayed back against the wall, out of the light and the smoke. His uncle stood with the other men around the boss, laughing and drinking. His uncle was smiling, but Danny didn't think he looked all that happy much. His cousins was standing with some of the older girls sweating in heavy dresses. Their collar-lace stuck to their throats and they peeled it back slow. The ladies fanned and had some drinks. The boys fought with each other to make them smile. His uncle looked up, and his cousins stopped till he was looking away again.

Danny could hear one of the ladies say it was too hot, and she started for the door. She had her shoes off and the bottom edge of her dress dragged over the spears of hay. One of his cousins followed her out. The other two kept gabbing with the ladies, but Danny didn't have no mind for that, so he stayed where he was. A cousin walked in front of him leading a woman by the hand, and they went to the back of the barn.

Danny got brave after a bit, and he walked over to the railcar. There was a lot of people in the way. He squeezed up the steps, wedged himself between the legs of the railcar men, heat and fish smell getting inside his clothes and skin. There was a shelf above him with paper plates, and he pulled one down and held it up to the fryer man. The man dumped some fish on it, and the line carried Danny out. He sat down against the wall and ate with his fingers. His throat was dry, and he swallowed a lot to get it wet again. He could hear the water lapping down the sides of the barn, thought about clean cold water clinging to leaves, but he didn't think his uncle would like him getting dirty much.

The girl was beside him then. She had a beer bottle in her hand and asked if Danny wanted some. He was real thirsty, so he said he did, and she gave it to him. Danny squeezed up his face. She giggled. It's nasty, he said. Nasty.

She said she knew that, but it was all they had, except for whiskey, but that was even worse.

Danny felt bad then. He said, thank you a lot.

She said her name was Cara and asked what his name was.

He said that his name was Daniel Lowe, but that he went by Danny Lowe.

Cara laughed at that, and Danny wasn't sure why.

Then she shoved him hard, and ran off toward the back of the barn.

Danny put down the bottle and meant to get her. He looked over at his uncle first, saw him say something. Boss laughed so hard he drooled corn liquor down his shirt, bent over coughing and beating his leg with his fist.

Danny slipped off between the barn wall and the hay stacked up, a thin alley. There was crates of scrap iron, sagging boxes of welding rods, metal hulks lying all over, and Danny kept bumping into them in the dark. He followed the edge of the hay wall back, the barn getting cooler and darker, Cara's shape slipping along in front of him. Above, high on the bales, he heard a woman sighing and his cousin talking real low and quick, but he couldn't hear nothing they said.

Danny was older and faster, but the alley was narrow and she knew it better than he did. She stayed ahead of him, yelling and laughing, Danny too, deep in the back of the barn where there was only dark and rain-sound. Water came down through the blown open loft windows. Lightning dropped in the pasture, the whole back of the barn lit. In a second when nothing had a shadow, Cara grinned at Danny over her shoulder, eyes big and mud-colored and full of light, so tiny with her tangled yellow hair fanning out around her face when she turned back, her teeth pale and sharp. Years after, she'd haunt him that way, limned in heaven light.

Then it was dark again, and he followed her out into the dim murk on the other side of the barn. She run off through the party folk and Danny skidded and stopped when he felt his uncle looking at him. Danny acted like he didn't see him and put his hands in his pockets. He went to stand in the fish line again for a few minutes, turned back and kept looking for Cara.

Her back was to him, and Danny saw she was looking for him, and he felt good. His uncle was talking, and most of the other people didn't see nothing below their belts. Danny came up behind and tumbled into her, grabbing her arms and saying, got you, gruff as he could and grinning.

He broke away this time, letting her dirty-warm hands go all at once, and sprinted off like hell was after him and not just some girl excited to get a turn at chasing. He slowed down going past Boss and his men, but didn't see his uncle nowhere. He took off down the barn wall again in the dark. She was lagging a little, and Danny slowed some just to show her he could, when he tripped on a sling and went down.

She pounced on him giggling, then jumped up and asked if he was okay. Danny said he was. They looked at each other a minute in the dark, breathing fast and happy to be together, and Danny asked if she wanted to go dance. She said, come on, and shot off.

Danny chased after like he was supposed to. They came out of the alley and into the party again, like coming up from water. They held hands and made up some fine dances, wearing out one a minute and laughing at it all. He kept staring at her muddy eyes, the rest of the room spinning around and going out of focus. The fiddler went fast or slow, depending on what the two of them did, and Cara kept moving to trip him up. They was all laughing, fiddler too, and

Cara shook so hard she fell down. She looked up at Danny then and smiled, and he wanted to keep it just like that always, her dark eyes and bright hair and crooked-sharp teeth.

He felt two hands squeeze him hard on the shoulders. His uncle and Boss was both standing there. They was drunk pretty good, Boss's eyes half closed. His uncle's grip was iron. The fiddler started a new set and shuffled away. Cara got up and smoothed down the front of her dress, brushing the hay off.

Boss asked what the hell she was doing carrying on with strange boys. He ain't family, Boss said, and said it again. He asked what she was doing running around like that. He asked if she wanted to be a whore like that sister of hers was, well did she. His eyes was flat and gray as clouds.

His uncle said he was sure it was Danny's fault. Danny looked at Cara crying and said, yeah, it was.

Cara said no it wasn't, that she'd started it.

Danny said it was all his idea and that they was just playing tag in the back of the barn, but not nothing else, and that he was sorry.

Boss cussed Danny for the conniving little shit that he was, and told his uncle he needed to do better by his own. His uncle nodded, face empty. Boss pulled his daughter away, and Danny's uncle took him by the arm.

They walked to the door, Danny's arm aching from where his uncle had him. Outside, just the storm and no cousin or girl. His uncle shoved Danny against some scrap tin leaning on the barn wall. The tin was wet and cold, and it filled his nose with its metal-smell. His uncle held him pinned to the wall by his throat and worked at getting his belt off with his other hand.

I told you, he said. I goddamn told you.

Danny said he was sorry over and over, but he knew it wouldn't do no good.

His uncle went to hitting him with the belt, all up and down from his neck to his legs. Danny hollered, and there was lightning, and there was wind, and there was water.

Finally, he let him go. Danny fell against the wall, sore to his bones. His uncle looked real sad, but he didn't know why yet. His uncle told him to walk back to the house and get to bed, and that he'd beat him near to death if he caught Danny sneaking around.

Danny walked stiff down the orange-mud road back to his uncle's house. Ruins of railcars gaped in the pasture across from him. The sky exploded over his head again and again. Rain passed down his face and back like hands, until he was numb all the way through and couldn't feel the belt no more. He was so wet, he didn't mind the puddles, but fell right through them, going in a straight line. He kept wanting her, how she'd been there in the barn when she'd turned around to see him, not knowing yet that he was never going to see her again. Years later, he'd think of her, how she'd done something to him, he didn't know what.

THORNS

THE STICKMAN'S CAGES

THE VILLAGERS HEARD the stickman coming before they saw him: hiss on the gravel road into town, the click and clack of branch to branch. He walked up the dirt street dragging bundles of wood and brier behind him. The stickman was twice as tall as the tallest man in the village and wore a cloak of brown leather, so patched it looked made of mouse skins. He was filthy and thin, vermin walking the blades of his straw-yellow hair and beard.

The stickman sat down against the side of Nye's dry goods store and began twisting and snapping his branches. The villagers came out to look. They'd never seen anything like him. Nye felt sorry for the stickman and asked him if he was hungry. The stickman kept twisting sticks in his long fingers. She brought him bread and put it in his lap. He ate it while they tried to get him to talk and wondered where he came from. Had the villagers left him alone, the stickman probably would have left. But they fed him, and because they fed him, he stayed.

The next morning, the stickman had made tiny globes of knitted branches and twine and placed one in front of every door. Inside each was a songbird, trilling mournfully. The villagers picked up their globes and stuck their fingers inside to brush the bright feathers. The birds panted and thrashed against the walls, loose feathers collecting in the bottom of the cage. The villagers laughed at the birds for being so afraid, and agreed that the cages were beautiful. Nye embraced him, startled that a body could be so hard and coarse, like a tree. Maybe then the stickman would have left. But they praised his cages, and because they praised him, he stayed.

All night, the villagers lay in their beds and listened to the warp and snap of branches. They heard the heavy tread around their doors and saw the stickman's shape blacken their windows as he walked by. They wondered what beautiful things he'd have for them tomorrow.

The next morning, Nye found her four cats rolling around on the porch inside globes of twisted branches. They saw her and ran to her feet, bumping the wood against her shins, meowing and clawing at the sides. Nye laughed at the stickman's joke. Outside, the other villagers found dogs, pigs, and chickens all rolling across the dirt in their round wooden cages. The villagers laughed, but when they tried to break them open, they couldn't. The branches would bend when twisted, but always bounced back to shape. They were too hard to saw through. The carpenter shook his head and said that they were clever things. While they talked about it, a boy rolled into the street in his cage, looking out at them through the bars. Everyone was quiet.

They found the stickman outside the village twisting together huge cages, bigger than any of the others. They couldn't make him understand that they wanted him to let the boy go. Nye picked at a half finished cage, and a pair of branches slid apart and sprang open towards her. She tried to fix it, but couldn't. The stickman kept working as though no one was there.

The villagers spent all afternoon working on the boy's cage with axes, knives, and metal bars. Nothing worked. The father told the boy to press himself to the back of the cage, then touched fire to the thinnest branch. The fire caught and swept over the globe, soaking it in flames. The branches bent but did not break as the father shook them, burning his hands. Afterward, everyone said that the boy had not screamed. The flames died out eventually, only ash and bone inside. The cage was blackened, but whole. The carpenter shook his head and said that they were clever things. Nye pulled the bones out of the cage, and they buried them. The villagers came to the stickman again. They told him that he would have to leave and take his cages with him. Smiling, he kept working on his row of giant globes.

That night, the villagers dreamed they were up high in a tree and couldn't climb down. While they dreamed, the stickman went to every window, leaned inside, and gathered the sleeping villagers in his arms. They awoke the next morning in round cages, the sun fractured through the wall of branches in front of them. Nye saw that the inside of the cage was lovely, the wood gleaming and white, the weave seeming to have no beginning or end. She found strange writing carved all along the inside and ran her finger over it, wondering what it meant.

The villagers were afraid. They shouted for the stickman to let them go. He tipped their barrels of rain water into the dirt street, turning it to mud. He rolled the wooden globes, airy and light, until they were coated, the mud dripping down through the gaps and soaking the villagers. Then he pushed them through the barn until they were covered in hay. The villagers lay in the egg-like dark and said nothing, their ears pressed against the damp walls.

Outside, the day was bright and green. A wall of wind came from the east and started the cages to rolling. The stickman led his cages to places none of them had been before. Inside her globe, Nye saw a gap in the wood, the place where she'd undone the branches the day before. She pushed against it, and the side of the cage opened and split. Nye shoved her body through, dried chips of mud falling like egg-shell, and fell out on the ground.

Her cage tumbled faster without her, catching up to the stickman in front. He did not look for her. The stickman climbed inside Nye's broken cage and started knitting it back together from within. The globes whispered over the grass and rushed away. Nye ran after them to help the others, but they were too fast and disappeared over the hills.

Nye looked for the stickman and his cages for years, wandering into lands she'd never heard of. The people there spoke languages she couldn't understand,

and eventually she gave up trying to speak to them at all. Her clothes wore thin, and Nye patched them with whatever she could find. She collected fallen branches and vines from the woods, dragging them behind her into villages. These, she twisted into small globes and gave to people, hoping that they would recognize them and point her in the direction of the stickman and everyone she loved. They were delighted, but did not understand. She slept in the shade of their houses, and they brought her bread. Sometimes, she left the small globes on their doorstops out of gratitude. Sometimes, birds would perch on them and fall inside, getting trapped. Nye picked up her sticks and headed to the next town, sure that she was getting closer.

The Hairdresser, the Giant, and the King of Roses

WHEN SHE WAS A STUDENT at Thomasville High, everyone could see that Marti Shepherd would be famous some day. She built dangerous science projects for school, steam engines and rocket launchers and laser arrays that had to be disposed of by the fire department. She baked cakes in the middle of the night, rolled stones into her parents' yard and chiseled them into Buddhas, tamed a possum, and never went to the same church twice. There was a rumor that she didn't believe in underwear, and thinking about whether or not this was true took up some boys' whole summers. Her hair was thick and blond with curl at the ends, and other girls concocted dyes in their kitchen sinks and burned themselves on curling irons trying to imitate it. When she was a teenager, she won the state beauty pageant. A man came and took her photo, and a picture of her in her crown was put up on a billboard outside of town: *Thomasville: City of Roses and Home of Miss Teen Georgia 2002.* She was a girl who had an amazing future, until it was taken away from her and she became a hairdresser.

The day after her high school graduation, an old witch knocked on Marti's parents' door and asked to speak to their daughter. Witches were common as preachers in Georgia, and they saw what she was right away. But her parents let the old woman in without questions. They were used to people wanting to see Marti.

Marti was in her room, packing for college, when the old woman came in and sat on her bed. The witch wore a gray dress that did not fit her well and combed through her greasy gray hair with thick fingers. "Always," the witch said, "It's about other people. They beat on my door because the baby has a rash, or they want a baby, or someone else has a baby who shouldn't. Dogs are missing. Rent is going up. The city won't refund the water deposit. Do they really need a baby or a water deposit? Will it make their lives better? Probably not. But they still come. It's never about me, is it?"

Marti looked at her walls, covered in track trophies, academic certificates, and art contest ribbons. "I can't imagine that," she said. "It's always been about me."

The witch smiled. "Which do you think is better? To live only for yourself, or to live only for others?"

Marti Shepherd was a sharp girl, and she knew a test when she saw one. The right answer was obviously to live for others, even if she really dreamed of leaving Thomasville, starring in movies, visiting India, having her name echo from one end of the world to the other. Her future stretched out before her, wide and deep and silver with possibility.

"Living for other people," Marti said with confidence. "That has to be more fulfilling."

"Then you can have it," the witch said. "Stay here and help people, and I'll go off and live for myself."

The witch touched Marti on the head, and the teenager felt the old woman take something from her.

Marti was dizzy. "Help people how?"

"Don't they ask you for things?"

She shrugged. "People ask me how I do my hair sometimes."

"Then you'll help them with their hair." With that, the strange old woman left.

That evening, the college called and said that there had been a mistake. Marti's admission was denied. She unpacked her things, sat on her bed, and stared at her feet, twisting the ends of her hair and wondering what she would do. As she pulled it through her fingers, her hair became heavier. Marti kept twisting her hair and watched it become gold in her hands. It was pleasantly heavy, and the metallic hair crashed against itself and swung like chains when she moved her head, sparkling in the light.

When her mother's friends came over, they surrounded Marti and ran their fingers through it.

"How did you do it?" they asked.

Marti didn't want to admit that she didn't know. She washed her hands in the sink, sat them down on barstools in the kitchen, and went through their hair with her fingers. As she worked their hair, it became gold under her hands. The women couldn't get enough of their reflections, clustering around the toilet and staring into the bathroom mirror until almost midnight.

The next morning, people were outside waiting, wanting the same. Marti resigned herself to life in Thomasville, at least for a little while, and applied for a job as a hairdresser. All the girls in town came to have her spin their hair into gold. One of the girls, a few years younger than Marti, turned and shook out her waves of heavy golden hair, neck straining with its weight. "Look," the girl said. "Even prettier than yours. And you were a beauty queen." Marti smiled at the girl, helped her out of the chair, and decided that she would never turn her own hair into gold again.

After a few years, Marti rented her own salon. The girls took their golden hair and did amazing things. Marti collected magazines with the girls' pictures on the covers, watching them appear on news programs or star in sitcoms. Always when they were interviewed, they thanked their hairdresser back home. Marti watched the tiny TV hanging in the corner, smoked cigarettes, and hoped for bad things to happen to them.

After taking Marti's future, the witch left Thomasville and was accepted to art school. She did one college play, then dropped out and moved to Hollywood. She met her agent in a bar and became his lover. She starred in movies with dancing, directed films, and came out with a swimsuit line. The witch rode Marti's future and knew that nothing in the world would ever make her give it up.

Years before the witch came, back when Marti was just a kid, a man named Ricky Long became a construction tycoon in Thomasville. Ricky was a broad man with a long beard and small, mean gray teeth. He was obsessed with roses. The year Marti graduated high school, Ricky had started digging deep moats around every piece of property he owned and filling the moats with thorny rose bushes. At first, it was only his ranch house and his construction office. Then a few apartment buildings. Some shopping strips. Gradually, Ricky Long began buying up all the property in town, surrounding it with roses so that everyone would know it was his.

From inside Ricky's buildings, old men gathered under flattened hats with cigars in their mouths. They spat blots of tobacco into empty coke bottles, listened to the whir and knock of aging ceiling fans above their heads, and watched vines climb the windows outside, blocking out the light, until they felt like they were Ricky's too. He had owned them, and he owned their kids, and they were afraid that he would own their grandchildren. They met in dairy bars and pool halls, islands surrounded by red roses, to chew on their hate for him, sliding their false teeth around in their mouths and wondering when someone would stand up to Ricky.

They thought that someone would be Bryan Cox. Bryan was the same age as Marti, in the same class. He moved to town from out of state, so there was that. But the main reason people expected big things from Bryan was because Bryan was big. When he moved to Thomasville at twelve, he was already a giant, bigger than every teacher at school. The old men came to his first football game and crowded in the stands, smiling in their red and white striped windbreakers. They held out their hands to measure his head and shoulders, compared his height to things they knew, like birdhouses, pine trees, and eighteen-wheelers. Here was someone who could do anything, they believed. But for over an hour, they watched Bryan fumble the ball and collect penalties. Everything he did was wrong, and big as he was with those stadium lights coming down on him, there was no way he could hide from it. Disappointed, the old men filed out of the stands and back to their Volkswagen van outside, not wanting to see their hero lose.

When he graduated, everyone knew that Bryan was good for nothing, all ten feet of him, and he couldn't find work anywhere in town. Only Ricky Long would hire him. No one could avoid seeing Bryan, and Ricky liked to think that when people saw Bryan, they would think of Ricky. So he came to the door of Bryan's mother's house and handed her a check. Bryan and his mom stayed in the house and paid rent, while Ricky's trucks pulled up in the yard and swallowed the old house with roses. Ricky hired the giant to put in the rose beds for him around town, slow and hot work that kept him by the roadside all day, where everyone could see.

The old men pulled up beside Bryan day after day, sitting in their van eating burgers and shaking their heads. "He could kill Ricky horrible," one of the old men said. "Might even look like an accident." "He could step on his head and crack it like a chicken egg," said another. "He could shake Ricky's hand and tear his arm right off." "And then beat him with it!" someone shouted. They watched Bryan work and fantasized about how he could ruin Ricky, kill him or run him out of town or just stand up to him, just one time not let him have his way. Frustrated, they threw empty soda cups down in the trench where Bryan was working. He knew what they wanted, but Bryan couldn't risk anything happening to his mother, and he didn't want to lose his job. He tucked his head, kept working, and hoped that they would give up on him.

Just as they did every few months, Ricky Long and his family came into Marti's beauty parlor to have their hair done. His wife and seven daughters all had dark hair that barely touched their shoulders, the tips of it shining with gold. Marti worked her hands through the hair of each of the eight women, tugging it until black became gold in her hands, and the hair lay heavy and bright on their heads. Ricky kicked back in one of her chairs, gray teeth grinning, and waited for her to touch up his beard, which was long and golden and curled down onto his chest.

The next day, Ricky walked into the coffee shops and hardware stores, his beard shining gold, braided into thick chains. The old men left their steaming coffee and doughnuts on the tables and walked out.

Ricky's daughters went to school, their hair cropped down almost to the scalp, their heads round and golden and shaved like monks. Ricky stuffed the heavy hair into envelopes and mailed it off to a Cash for Gold company. His wife did not leave the house for months, not until her hair had grown back out. When that happened, Ricky would lead his sad family back to the salon, and Marti would have to turn their hair into gold again.

Marti came to work one morning and found a white truck parked on the sidewalk of the shopping center. The truck read, *Long Landscaping*, on the side. In the bed was a stack of white lattice and pots on pots of rose bushes. Bryan was digging a moat all around the store, working a heavy coal shovel in each broad hand.

"What are you doing?" Marti asked.

It had been almost ten years since the two of them had been in school together. She was still the woman on the billboard outside of town: blond hair curling over her shoulders, big brown eyes, sharp white teeth, and freckles scattered over the bridge of her nose. She had been nice to him in school. He knew that she would not be his friend today.

"Ricky bought the whole shopping center this morning," Bryan said.

"I don't want those damn things around my salon."

From the parking lot, the old men sat up in their van and listened through the open windows. Maybe she would push him into doing something, they hoped. Beautiful women could do that. The old men waited, barely breathing.

Bryan looked at the dirt. "It's Ricky's salon," he said.

The old men swore and honked the horn, their hands shaking so bad that they dropped their cigarettes. Years they'd watched Bryan. Years he'd failed them.

Marti went to Bryan's truck, the seats torn out and top peeled open to make room for him. She'd seen him riding around town, head sticking out of the top, left arm and shoulder squeezed out the window, knees to his chest. She reached into the truck bed, raised a potted rose bush over her head, and smashed it on the asphalt. Bryan hunched his great shoulders and turned away from her, keeping to his work.

All afternoon, Marti spun hair into gold for girls going to prom. She imagined the pictures, a crowd of girls with the same golden hair. Outside her windows, arms of white lattice fell against the glass and the heads of roses stuck up from the trench. Bryan sweated in the sun, his long hair dirty and hanging in his face.

When it slowed down in the afternoon and she had no more appointments, Marti went outside. She touched Bryan on the arm, stopping his shoveling. "You need a break," she said.

"Okay." Bryan looked around. He started to sit.

"Come inside," Marti said. "There's air conditioning."

He tried to make himself small as he came through the door, standing in the middle of the room so that he wouldn't knock over any furniture accidentally.

Marti gestured to the floor beside one of her stools.

Bryan came over and sat. Sitting, they were the same height. Marti was staring at his hair and face, biting her bottom lip. Bryan was conscious of the dirt smudged into his work shirt and jeans, caked on the bottoms of his boots. He remembered a rumor that she had something against underwear.

Marti tipped his head back into the sink and started to wash his hair. "You look good with long hair," she said. "But it's dirty. And it needs to be cut."

"People don't usually notice my hair," he said.

"I noticed it."

Water rushed over his head, pooling in his ears. Her face was very close to his, leaning over him to work, and he closed his eyes. He felt her breath on his forehead. Her fingertips probed his scalp. She smelled clean, like new soap or shampoo. For a few minutes, the whole world was her.

She dried his hair and started to trim it even.

"Thank you," Bryan said. "For treating me like a normal person."

Marti was quiet for a while, working her scissors and comb, and Bryan worried that he'd said something wrong.

On the tiny TV, the witch was exploring Roman tombs by torchlight, a beautiful and shirtless man holding her close.

"In school, I always thought it would be terrible to be normal. But I don't mind it."

"You could never be normal," Bryan said.

On TV, Nazis cornered the witch and the man, and he leaned in to kiss her passionately before they dragged him away. Marti turned the TV off.

"I'm going to color your hair," she said.

Bryan looked worried. "Not gold."

"It's what I do, big guy. Sit still."

"If you make my hair gold, Ricky will take it."

"He wouldn't dare," Marti said. "No one would take something from a guy like you."

Bryan left the salon with his hair swinging and golden, sparkling in the sun, the feel of Marti's hands and her smell staying with him. He kept working the rest of the afternoon, old men driving by in their van and noticing a change in him. The girl had done something. They saw Bryan's golden hair and knew that if he could just say no to Ricky, if even one person refused to give the man what he wanted, they would be satisfied.

The next day, Marti waited for Bryan to come back and keep working on the moat of flowers. She had appointment after appointment, watching the window as she pulled hair through her fingers. By evening, she locked her door, got in her silver Kia, and drove around town. Bryan was not a man who could hide. She would see him or she would see his truck. There were no others like them.

She found him sitting on a bench in the square, taking up the whole thing by himself, his legs blocking the sidewalk. A crowd of old men were gathered around him. They yelled in his face, hocked up tobacco spits on his wide shoes, and swore at heaven. What would it take to move him, they wondered. Could anything do it?

Marti pulled up beside him and saw that his hair was gone, shaved down to the skin. "I gave that to you," she said.

Bryan kept his eyes down. "Ricky Long owns my mother's house," he said. "We just rent. Every morning when I wake up, the sun comes red through the roses outside my window."

Marti drove away, leaving Bryan at the mercy of the old men. She thought about the roses growing up the windows of her salon, imagined them taking the whole building, blocking the roads, covering the sun. She went to find the witch.

The witch's old cottage had been bulldozed years ago and a mansion built on the land. It stood across the road from the billboard of seventeen year old Marti Shepherd, Miss Teen Georgia 2002. The witch's house had a wrought iron fence around it and an intercom at the gate.

After trying the intercom and getting no one, Marti climbed over the fence and started walking across the lawn. A pack of Dobermans ran out to her, but they were young and had been neglected by the witch, who was rarely home. They fell against Marti's legs, licking her feet and begging for love. She pet them and left golden palm prints across their fur. They followed her all the way to the front door.

Inside, the walls were covered in movie posters from all the witch's films. Marti found her on the couch with a fleet of aging action stars, the men struck dumb by steroids and camera flashes, taking turns massaging the witch's great feet and talking about sandwiches. They listed their favorite ingredients: raspberry jelly, shaved radish, sweet pickles, teriyaki chicken, honey mustard.

"Marti, you beautiful thing," the witch said. She stood and hugged her. "That future of yours is just getting warmed up. Next year, I'll be modeling lingerie on the moon."

"I need it back," Marti said. "I'm sorry, but what you gave me isn't helping people at all."

"You can't actually help them. You give them what they ask for, but it never makes anything better. I thought I made that clear."

"Ricky Long is using me to ruin people's lives. I don't want to turn hair into gold anymore."

The witch frowned. "Gold isn't good enough for you? Fine. Turn hair into anything you like. See if you can come up with something better."

"That's not what I wanted," said Marti.

But the witch wasn't listening. She sat back down on the couch between the action stars. They passed a plate of finger sandwiches around, no two alike, placing small triangles in the witch's mouth. The witch chewed, raised her feet, and wiggled her toes at them.

For the next few weeks, Marti tried to stop turning hair into gold. People came from all over town, begging her to do their hair, but she said no. They left long and rambling messages on her voice mail, telling her how selfish she was. When she ran out of money, Marti called people to apologize. She went back to the salon and pulled golden hair through her fingers for days.

While she worked, Marti watched Bryan bring roses and wrap them around the lattice, raising walls of red petals on the window glass. His hair was starting to come back, touching the tops of his ears. The old men sat in their van all day in the parking lot, windows cracked to vent heat and smoke. They imagined their funerals, the coffins covered by a wave of roses, thorns climbing the cemetery fence, vines burying them forever.

In the evenings, Marti gathered up the hair clippings from the day and practiced. She held fistfuls of pine straw and feathers, rubbed them between her hands until she knew their feel, and started twisting hair into new shapes. When teenagers came into Marti's salon to have their hair done, she asked, "How about feathers? Plastic? Scales?"

"We want gold," they said.

One morning, the bell over the door rang, and Ricky Long led his family into the store. The women's hair just touched their necks. Ricky lined them up on Marti's stools, smiling with his small gray teeth. Outside, Bryan stumbled against the salon's glass windows, leaving a thick crack running across the face of the store.

Marti did the wife's hair, running it through her fingers until it became gold. She turned the chair so that the wife could see herself in the mirror, bent down to the woman's ear, and whispered, "When you look in the mirror tomorrow, you will look like this."

She did the oldest daughter's hair and said the same, then the next oldest, and the next, until she had done them all. Only Ricky Long was left. He spread out in the salon chair and waited for her, a few inches of white at the top of his beard, the rest golden and bright.

She started by running her hands over his head. His white hair was thick, and he usually kept it short. It was a little over an inch long now.

"Why haven't we given you gold on top?" Marti asked him.

Ricky smiled. "Miss Georgia," he said.

The first time she'd met him, Marti was fifteen. She'd been at a Mexican restaurant in town with her parents, celebrating making it into the pageant. Their food had just arrived, and Ricky walked in, his clothes dusty with white sheetrock powder. He went from table to table, asking everyone how the food was, the cooks and waiters watching him and not speaking. "This is our daughter," Marti's mother had said. Ricky had gestured to the window. "This is my town."

Marti lowered his chair so that she was well above him. "Teen Georgia," she said. "I never made it any further than that." She combed through his hair and beard. The light coming in from the window was tinged the color of roses. Bryan's shadow cut across the room.

"We should make the top match," she said.

"I'll just clip it short," said Ricky. "Not worth the money or the time."

"We could make it look like a crown," Marti said. "Just shape it a little."

Ricky thought about it, his daughters and wife staring at him, wondering what Marti was doing. He pulled a golden coil out of his pocket, the hair he had taken from Bryan, and played with it in his hand.

"If anyone should have a crown," he finally said, "it ought to be me." He put the coil of hair back in his pocket.

Marti turned him away from the mirror and began. She teased his hair up, twisting it into long stems, the little hairs sticking off the stems becoming barbs. Under her hands, Ricky's golden beard and his hair became green and tough. She pulled at the hair where it emerged from his scalp, making it root-like and hard.

"What are you doing?" Ricky asked.

"You like roses, so I gave you roses," Marti said. She lifted her hands, wet with blood from the thorns.

Ricky turned to see the mirror, but when he moved, the long tangle of thorny vines cut into his neck and cheeks. He shoved his hands into the thorns and pulled, but they were rooted deeply in his skin. Every time he moved, every time he breathed, the thorns savaged him. Ricky fell out of the chair and ran from the salon with petals streaming behind him, out across the parking lot with no destination, his whole head filled with the pain of his roses.

The old men dropped their soda bottles of warm tobacco juice and let them roll on the floor. Ricky Long, a thick rose bush surrounding his head, ran in front of them.

With a shout, the old men chased after him in their van, honking at Ricky and throwing garbage. They got out and stuck a birthday hat on his head, took turns holding up their camera phones and posing for pictures with him, cackling with delight.

"You should go get him," Marti told the Long women. They filed out to collect their father and take him home where the old men couldn't abuse him.

Bryan stood at the door, a shovel in his hand. "What now?" he asked.

Marti pointed at the trench running around the shopping center. "Now we fill that back in." Marti grabbed another shovel out of the work truck and stood beside him, helping Bryan cover the moat. They buried the roses under black dirt.

"I don't need any help," he said, "but I like you being here."

"I'm not going anywhere," she said.

Bryan watched her struggle beside him, covering over the flowers, and he knew that Ricky would do his best to run her out of town. He'd close down the shopping center, buy up all the salons in town, do whatever he could to make sure that there was no place for Marti here.

When they were done, Marti took him into the salon and washed his hair, turning it to gold again. "Keep it this time," she said, "so people will know that you're mine."

The next day, Bryan drove to the Long family's ranch house on the outside of town. His daughters answered, their faces warm and happy, their hair long for the first time in years. They took him through the house, Bryan walking stooped over with his arms close to his sides, until they reached the door to Ricky's home office. The girls left him there, hurrying away from their father.

Bryan walked into a room overtaken with roses. They snaked over the floor and climbed the walls, leafy and flowering. At the ceiling, they burrowed under the tiles and wound themselves around the rafters. The curtains in the room were torn down, letting sunlight fall fully on Ricky Long, who sat in the middle of the floor, all the roses growing from his head.

Ricky didn't move, but his small eyes swiveled up to see the giant. "That golden hair," Ricky said. "Give it to me."

Bryan shook his head.

"Oh? A shame to have to raise the rent on your mom's place."

"You'll leave my mom alone. And you won't try to run Marti Shepherd out of town."

At the mention of her name, Ricky jerked his head, the thorns biting into his neck. "Why won't I?"

"Because if you leave her alone, I'll keep working for you. And any time someone sees me in town, they'll know I'm yours. Now that you'll be staying home, you need that more than ever."

Ricky sighed, bowing his head under the weight of the vines. He told Bryan where he wanted him to be the rest of the week.

That afternoon, the Long girls were crowded onto the back of the school bus, listening to the other kids whisper. They'd heard that Ricky Long had gone crazy and wouldn't go outside anymore. That his construction company was coming apart. They wanted to ask the girls if it was true, that their father had lost his mind. But outside the bus windows, they could see Bryan working with those big hands, tending rose beds or collecting rent, his shadow falling over the windows. "You leave those girls alone," someone said. "They have a giant."

Up and down the roads of Thomasville, the old men drove in their sputtering van. For the next couple of years, they watched Long's businesses fold. His family sold property, and the moats of roses fell back to the edges of the city. He still owned a few things, but the old men wouldn't have to see their grandkids work for him. They sat in dairy bars, doughnut shops, coffee places, and gas stations, looking out through clean windows. Their stories were about Marti Shepherd.

GUN JUGGLING

THIS IS THE WAFFLE HOUSE where the jugglers live. Through the grease-smeared door, the cashier tumbling receipts and rolls of change above the register. Pancakes, eggs, sausages making tight orbits in the air over the kitchen. Clean plates spinning dry and tossed onto their stacks. The floor rolling with tennis balls, colored scarves, boiled eggs, dozens of dropped things. Eric, head cook and master juggler, reigns here in clean apron and hairnet, thin blond mustaches twisted with citrus pomade.

The walls are spotted with patched bullet holes, all the windows cracking and held together with strips of window tint. Gunpowder in the air, lingering beneath syrup and bacon smell. All this because of Mel, criminal and greatest juggler Eric ever trained.

Eric stands at the front and calls everyone to come and listen. He juggles with elbows raised, spatulas making lazy spins between his palms. They rise and fall with his chest, natural as breathing. He lets the spatulas pile up on the counter, stacked alternating, their ends dripping oil. He is calm, the way a juggler should be.

The servers come, the seated customers with syrup and honey on their lips, the cashier, assistant cooks, the dishwasher. "I've taught you everything I can," Eric tells them. "It's time I left the Waffle House."

The dishwasher raises his hand. "But you promised to tell us about the bullet holes, the cracked glass, everything that happened here years ago, before we were hired."

"All right," says Eric. "Listen. I'll tell you about me and Mel."

It was the middle of summer, and the circus hadn't been pulling in enough money. The ringleader told Eric he was sorry, but there would have to be cuts. "People have YouTube," the ringleader told him. His eyes were full of these fears: wireless signal floating through the air and into his head, a smart-phone in every pocket, digital eight-second clips of lion-taming or tight-rope walking, anything that was free. The ringleader cleaned the sweat from his bald head with a tissue. "No one comes to the circus to see juggling anymore."

Eric hugged his apprentice, Mel, tiny girl with lanky arms and legs, brown hair down her back, just turned seventeen. "We understand," Eric said. "If people won't come to see juggling, we'll bring juggling to them."

The ringleader wished them luck.

Down the highway with everything they had in a backpack, summer sun hot on their heads. Mel sat on the shoulder and beat her palm on the asphalt. "I hate him," she said. "I hate every damned ringleader."

Eric held up his hand and watched eighteen-wheelers roll by. "Jugglers can't hate, Mel. It'll make you drop things."

Mel wiped her eyes and nodded. She pulled knitted bean bags out of her pocket and started to juggle them. "Stay calm," she told herself. "Even after all this, stay calm." She put all three in the air, tossing them underhand, trying to keep her arms limp and lazy.

Eric smiled. "Your shoulders are tense. You're trying too hard."

A van full of children slowed down, kids' faces pressed to the glass watching Mel juggle on the roadside. Mel thought they were going to stop, heard the brakes squeaking, but the car started speeding up again once they had seen.

Mel caught the balls one by one as they came down and threw them at the car, one hitting the bumper and splitting open, one skipping over the road and getting run over by a car, and the last one rolling into the thick grass in the median. The van honked at them as it disappeared. Eric stared at the ruin of the beanbags.

"I'm sorry," Mel said. "I just lost control."

"It's not about control." Eric pulled out a handful of thin scarves, red and green and blue. "It's about peace. You just have to relax." He tossed the scarves up overhand, letting them drift back down, and cycled them up again. The wind pulled them to the side, and Eric walked down the road with them, letting himself be carried. His movements were sleepy, a slow stirring in the air.

Mel watched him and shook her head. When she juggled, even on her best days, it looked like she was punching the air. A few more cars passed, and finally another family stopped. Mel and Eric squeezed in between their kids in the backseat.

"Where are you headed?" the woman asked them.

"Where are you headed?" Eric asked.

"There's a Waffle House a few miles up the road. We're stopping for lunch."

"That sounds fine," Eric said. "You can drop us off there."

In the Waffle House, Eric and Mel tossed packets of jelly and sugar across the table, each making half of an elliptical pattern. The restaurant was quiet, everyone listening to the smack of paper and plastic against their palms, watching the jugglers play.

"There's never been anything like this," the manager said. "Not in any Waffle House anywhere." He paid for their lunch. The family who'd picked them up told everyone how they had brought the jugglers. The manager paid for their food too.

"What did *they* do?" Mel said it quietly, looking down at the table so only Eric could hear.

"What do any of us do?" Eric asked her, but Mel didn't know what he wanted her to say, why he didn't understand, so she said nothing.

Eric got up to buy a roll of pennies from the cashier. After she gave it to him, he asked, "Are there any tennis courts around here?"

Eric and Mel sat in the grass outside the tennis court, watching yellow balls smack against the chain-link fence and waiting for some to make it over. They'd been there for a couple of hours.

"I feel like a little kid, waiting out here," Mel said.

Eric laughed and squeezed her shoulder. "You're a pro. The best I've ever taught."

Mel shrugged and said, "Thanks." Inside her head, she repeated his words over and over, that she was the best, burning with the truth of it and loving the feeling.

"Now you're smiling."

Eventually, worse tennis players came to the court, and Eric and Mel caught a small pile of stray balls. They were stacked in Mel's lap, a mound of fresh yellow Wilson's, still smelling store-new, when one of the players walked up to the fence and yelled at them.

"Hey," he said, "Thanks for finding those. But can we have them back now?"

Eric took them out of Mel's lap and started throwing them back over the fence, one by one.

"What are you doing? We've been out here for hours."

"There will always be more."

Mel threw the rest of the balls over the fence all at once. They bounced and rolled into other lanes, interrupting matches, while the man darted over the court to collect them, apologizing to everyone.

After a while, a landscaping crew rolled up and started mowing the lot behind the court. Mel and Eric moved to a bench while they worked. After the mowers left, it was almost dark. Eric went out to the grass.

"What are you doing?" Mel asked. "All the players are gone."

Eric waved to her, and Mel got up and walked over. With the grass cut short, she could see dozens of dirty yellow tennis balls, lopsided and split open from the lawn mower blades.

"Fine. You're right again." Mel picked out six of the best looking ones, and they filled the insides with pennies and wrapped them in black electrical tape from Eric's backpack. Mel tossed them up and let them fall heavy into her palm, liking the sound of pennies sloshing together inside. "They could be a little heavier," she said.

"Always twenty pennies in a tennis ball. You're just throwing them too hard. Throw them softer."

"Where are we staying tonight, Eric?"

"There's a motel across from the Waffle House. I thought we'd stay there a few nights, then see what else is in town. We've got money saved. I like the Waffle House."

Mel flipped up the bottom of her shirt to carry her six juggling balls, the tape shiny black under the park lights, and followed Eric. He picked up twigs, stones, and sweet-gum balls as they walked, juggling a column higher and higher. Surely he'll drop something soon, Mel thought, as Eric kept adding to the cloud of objects he had in the air, but he didn't. He walked along juggling, staring at the sky and picking up things to add effortlessly. She wondered if he knew he was doing it.

Eric and Mel spent a week finding things to juggle and bringing them back to the Waffle House. They went to the Little League field for baseballs. The Country Club for golf balls. To weddings of people they didn't know, lingering afterward to collect unwanted crepe paper and tulle for scarves, carrying off tiki lanterns to chop down into juggling pins and torches. Eric and the Waffle House manager made space in the freezer and storeroom for these things, staying up all night talking together. Eric began wearing an apron and hairnet, working in the kitchen. Mel spoke to him less and less, saw servers and dishwashers dropping plates and pawing at scarves. She didn't understand what was happening.

One day, she walked around the building and juggled while she waited for Eric to finish his shift inside. The balls still felt too light, and they crisscrossed higher and higher, until she lost control of them and they all came falling down. She was juggling five, and she knew that was part of the problem, but she was too proud to juggle less. It would feel like defeat, she thought, to have three in the air and juggle them perfectly.

Coming to the back of the building, she stood facing a wall of brick, concentrating on keeping all five going. They started to slip away, and Mel got angry, tossing them up faster and harder. She lost one, sent it soaring out of pattern and into the wall where it smacked like a change-purse against the brick and bounced back towards her. She barely caught it in her left hand, throwing the ball in her right at the wall too.

Then she had it, eight feet from the wall, throwing the balls as hard as she wanted, smacking them against the brick so that the sound echoed off the cars parked behind her, the balls bouncing back to her hands so she could send them whizzing at the wall. She'd never juggled so well before, and kept the pattern going for forty minutes, until her arms ached.

Mel walked back into the Waffle House and found Eric putting on a new name tag. It read, *Assistant Manager*. "What do you think?" he asked.

"I think you're the greatest juggler in the world. Why are you doing this?"

He smiled a sad smile, but didn't look up from his application. "You heard the ringleader, Mel. People don't pay to see juggling anymore."

"Maybe we could change things. Listen, I just figured something out. Behind the store a few minutes ago. You should have seen it. It was angry and happy and everything all at once. I was great, Eric. I had passion."

"Mel, you can't juggle with passion. You have to be calm. I've been telling you for years."

Mel looked at the restaurant tables, the servers trying to juggle, Eric's new uniform. She hated all of it, even him. Mel walked out of the restaurant, Eric calling for her to stop. He asked where she was going, but Mel didn't answer. She walked across the parking lot and followed the road towards the tall buildings sparkling in the sun downtown. Something good was waiting for her there, she decided. It had to be, after all this.

Downtown, Mel walked past cafés and clothing stores, a row of old factories that had been boarded up, a post office. She stopped outside of a tall building with gray columns and spreading concrete stairs. People went in and out of the building's six main doors. It reminded her of the circus where she'd spent most of her life, the towering main tent, the grandeur of the thick yellow ropes and snapping flags. She went in.

Inside, the floor was green marble with bronze edging the outermost tiles. There were more columns inside, clean wooden tables, and a counter with rows of people behind it along the back, like ticket-sellers. It was quiet.

Mel walked past a huge man, bull-like in his black coat and black cowboy hat, reaching into his coat pocket. Big Man stopped when he met her eyes, seeming embarrassed, and looked at the floor. Mel went to the woman behind the counter and asked what this place was.

"First National Bank." The woman had dark red nails and wore her blond hair up. "Do you have an account with us?"

"No. Sorry. I thought this was something else."

The woman laughed. "What were you expecting?"

Mel remembered crowds filling the tent, Eric juggling torches burning at both ends, keeping six in the air at once. Mel standing in front of him as a girl, the flames twirling around her and only kept back by his arms, her hair curling in the heat. Every eye on them.

Before Mel could answer the woman's question, someone screamed at the other end of the line.

Big Man leveled a fat revolver at the tellers. He tossed balled-up plastic sacks over the counter and said to fill them up. From the entrance, more men started pulling out guns, their hat-brims pulled down to shade their eyes from the cameras high along the walls.

Big Man shouted for everyone to get down, so Mel dropped to the floor, the tile cold on her hands. She heard someone shout, "Police!" There was gunfire, the sound of the shots echoing back from the ceiling. She heard people cry out, could taste the gunpowder in the smoky room. Everything was quiet then.

Mel lifted her head and saw the bodies of police officers and robbers strewn all over the bank. Big Man was sitting with his back to one of the columns, tearing a long strip from his shirt and tying it around his arm, his black coat sleeve sopping wet.

On the floor next to Mel, there was a dead cop, his gun cocked in his dead hand. Mel crawled towards it. What am I doing? she thought. She needed to stay still, be calm. That's what Eric would tell her to do. But she was afraid of Big Man, and she was angry at him for making her afraid. She picked up the gun, astonished at how perfectly heavy it was in her hand. She grabbed another one on the cop's belt, stood, pointed both of them at Big Man, and started walking towards him.

He looked at her, his revolver lying on the floor beside him, and kept wrapping his arm.

"Why did you do this?" she asked.

Big Man said, "Because I want the money."

"You can't just have whatever you want." Mel's eyes were wet. "You've got to have restraint."

Big Man looked at the girl, her wet bright eyes and tense body, and thought that he could love her. He stood, the barrels of her guns pressing into his chest, and pushed the hair back out of her eyes. "Who told you such a thing?" he asked.

The doors burst open, and Mel and Big Man turned their guns to the front of the building. More cops ran inside. "Get down!" one of the officers yelled.

"You don't have to do what they say," Big Man told her.

"I said, get down!"

"I don't know what to do," Mel told him. "What should I do?"

Big Man took a step away from her. "That's one thing I won't ever tell you."

The police kept shouting. Big Man was looking at her. She had both guns pointed at the cops. Mel let out the breath she'd been holding in and tossed her guns into the air, starting a pattern. It was the only thing she could do.

Big Man laughed and threw his revolver to her, Mel adding it to the rest. He pulled two more guns out of the back of his waistband and threw these to her too.

Mel had five guns flying up into the air and dropping back down to her palms, crossing them back and forth, switching between overhand and underhand patterns, catching one behind her back.

The police stared, wondering what they should do now, when they all heard the sound of a gun being cocked. Mel was pulling back the hammers as they fell into her left hand and throwing them into her right.

"Drop those," the cop said.

"I can't stop." Mel cocked two more. "You should all get down."

Big Man started laughing, a deep and wicked sound.

"Drop those, or I shoot!" another cop said. They all had their guns on Mel now.

She juggled the guns faster and faster, their hammers catching on her thumb and snapping back, the handles catching in her right hand with her finger on the trigger. Everything was lining up too perfectly. She couldn't help but pull it.

Mel strafed the bank with gunfire, sending shots up the legs of the columns and zipping across the lobby. The cops were carved with gunfire from every direction, shots hitting them straight on or bouncing off the walls. The bank employees and customers were on the floor, screaming. The only person standing besides Mel was Big Man. He watched her from under his hat, bullets striking the floor in front of him or squealing past his ear, but never hitting him.

"You're beautiful," he said. He threw extra clips into her pattern, watching Mel switch out the empties as she juggled them. "Don't let anyone stop you."

While Mel kept shooting, lost to her juggling, Big Man ran behind the counter and collected his bags half-filled with money. He took holsters from the police officers and tossed these to Mel, extra guns for himself. After she'd strapped the guns on, heavy and hot even through their cases, Big Man scooped her onto his shoulder and started for the door.

"I have a car around back," he told her.

Mel felt his thick shoulders and arms through his coat, careful not to touch the place where he'd been shot. "I can walk," she said.

The man shook his head and looked at her, worship all over his face. "Someone like you. Your feet should never have to touch the ground."

With sirens in the distance, Mel and the bank robber pulled up at the Waffle House. "I have to take care of something." She kissed his rough cheek.

Mel found Eric inside behind the counter.

"Where have you been?" he asked. "I was worried. Who is that man in the parking lot? Why do you have all those guns?"

Mel spread her arms so Eric could see each of the five pistols holstered on her body. "You told me it couldn't be done. But I'm here to show you what juggling with passion looks like."

She started throwing the guns into the air, and Eric yelled for everyone to get on the floor. Mel spun them on her finger, tossed them over her shoulder and under her leg, cocking and firing the guns without aiming, but never hitting anyone. She blew out the front windows, put holes in all the tables and counters, cracked the sheetrock on the walls. Her empties piled up on the floor, and it stank of gunpowder so badly when she finished that Eric could barely breath.

"You would have kept me from ever knowing I could do this."

Eric tried to speak, but Mel shushed him with a gun barrel laid against his lips.

"I killed people, Eric. It was easier that I thought it would be. Not nearly as hard as juggling." She looked around the shattered interior of the Waffle House. "I'm glad you like this place. If you ever leave, I'll kill you too."

Through a pane of broken glass, Eric watched her get into a long black car with the man and spin out of the gravel parking lot. He thought of her every day after that, with every new employee he taught to juggle in the Waffle House. Every night, wondering what he'd done so wrong.

"I haven't seen her since that day," Eric says. "They talk about her on TV or radio news sometimes. Hitting banks in California, last I heard."

Sunlight flares in the cracks in the windows, and Eric rotates two eggs in his palm. More people come inside, a troop of girl scouts in green and brown.

"So which is it?" the dishwasher asks. "What should jugglers have? Passion or restraint?"

"I'm going to go see Mel and find out," Eric says. "And if she kills me, there will be jugglers still."

They hug Eric goodbye one by one, and he steps through the door, tossing fresh eggs high into the air and letting them drop back into his palms lazy and gentle. He could do this forever. He would never break one.

ASH FLOWERS

SHAY OPENED HER FRONT DOOR and found the living room full of
flowers. The school bus sighed in the road behind her, its tires pulling against
the gravel road. Her backpack was heavy on her shoulders, and her shoelaces
were yellow and winding apart at her feet. She held the door half open, bundles
of tied flowers stacked behind it. Her mother and older sister talked in the back
of the house.

She came inside and set her backpack down on the floor. The couch was
covered in piles of pale irises, some in clay pots. Sheaves of long-stemmed roses
stuck out from underneath. There were four pots of flowers in her mother's
wingback chair, and petals and fallen leaves were scattered over the carpet. Her
father's recliner, green and broken-down in the seat, was the only empty space.

Shay went into the kitchen, pulling the petals between her fingers. Thin
black vases with shaggy-headed carnations stood on the table. In the sink, there
was a wreath of yellow flowers. A blue banner ran across it reading, *In Loving
Memory*. Shay stepped between the piles of flowers in the hallway, following the
sound of her sister's voice. They were in her parents' bedroom.

"He's gonna be pissed off," her mother said and laughed. Shay had never
heard her laugh like that before, a high, manic sound. Her mother was wearing
jean coveralls and her shoes were spotted with road-mud.

Shay's sister, Dana, slammed a vase down on the dresser. "He can be pissed. How long has it been since he did anything for you?"

Dana noticed Shay and pinched her ear too hard. "Hey, girl."

Shay reached out and put her hand on Dana's stomach, round and huge and hot, stretching out the front of her tank top. Shay had checked out three books on babies, and they were all in her backpack. She knew exactly what her niece looked like curled up inside Dana's belly, but her sister never cared about the books. Shay wished the baby could be hers instead.

"And every day at the nursing home, them old ladies get flowers from people," her mother said. "I have to watch them come in with vases all the time. Sometimes, they get flowers for no damn reason."

The phone rang in the kitchen, and Dana went to answer it.

Her mother looked at Shay. "No damn reason," she said again.

"Can I have some too?" Shay asked.

Her mother took a drink from a glass of iced tea on the dresser, flowers stacked up in the crook of her arm and nowhere to put them. "These are for me," she said. "It's past time I got something."

Shay nodded, sad.

"I guess you can have a few. Do you want these?" Her mother held out a flattened bouquet of roses, the stems broken off and uneven. The blooms were just starting to open, swollen at the base and cupping narrow at their tips. There were a black, bloody red.

Shay took them into the living room and got her backpack. Dana was scratching at her stomach with long fingernails and smacking gum into the phone. "No, he ain't made it home yet. I don't know what he's gonna say, but I need to stay here with Mama till he says it. No, I'm not gonna let him run me off."

Shay went into the laundry room. Against one wall, the washer and dryer clattered. Against the other, she had her bed and a trunk for her things, the wall painted purple on her side of the room. Shay set the flowers on her pillow. She wondered if she should put them in water maybe, but she liked how dark the roses looked against her bed.

Shay went back down the hall and asked her mother, "Why is Daddy gonna be mad?"

"Maybe he won't be, sweetie," her mother said. "Maybe he'll think it's funny." She laughed again, the same way.

"Because we stole them," Dana said. "You think somebody give us these?"

Her mother drained the rest of her glass, face red from being in the sun. "Maybe he'll think it's funny."

They stared at Shay, and she could tell they wanted to talk without her listening, so she went outside. It was still sunny and hot out, the grass thick and knifed with pine-needles. The yard sloped back into woods at one end and a pond on the other, but the weeds were too thick around the pond for Shay to be able to see the water.

She sat in the rusted swing set her father had welded together for her, the spot where the chain attached to the rubber seat biting into her thighs. Shay pumped her legs and lifted her body into the air, yellow shoelaces twirling. Once she got high enough, she could see the flat, white disc of the pond in the sunlight. The swing set rocked from her motion, its front legs lifting off the ground every time she swung back, stabbing back into the grass when she soared forward. There was nothing to do but wait.

Shay strained to see what was swimming across the skin of the pond, following the "v" of its body moving through the water and the black speck of its head, when clouds moved over the sun and the yard became dark. She knew that her father was home.

She let her feet drag in the dirt until she'd stopped swinging and ran to meet his car. Her father parked an old gray Civic next to the house and got out. He handed Shay things—an empty green coffee thermos, a newspaper, a sack of trash from his lunch. Her father's left cheek had a long scar from where he'd caught it on a piece of barbed wire before she'd been born. Every time she saw a fence, she thought of him. His shirt was spotted with dirty hand-prints, and his pants sagged against his wide leather belt, pockets stuffed with screwdrivers, pliers, and gloves.

"She made anything to eat?" he asked.

Shay shook her head.

"Your sister comes over and they get to carrying on. She forgets to cook. Now we have to wait to eat? You don't know, huh?"

He spat into the yard and closed the car door. Shay followed him into the house.

Her father looked at the flowers in the living room for a long time, but didn't say anything. The flowers pulled back under his eyes, the blooms tucking into hard, closed little buds. All across the room, they receded from him, the leaves rustling as they moved. The blue and white buds flushed dark, returning to green.

He cocked his head to listen, and Shay heard her sister ask, "Is he home?"

Her father walked through the kitchen, stopping so hard his shoes squeaked on the floor when he saw the wreath in the sink. "That's Jim Lowe's," he told Shay. "Do you remember Jimmy?"

Shay shook her head.

"His wife took care of you when you were a baby. We got pictures of Jimmy holding you." He looked down at her blank face, and Shay could see that he wanted her to say something, but she didn't know what. "Guess that was a long time ago," he said.

Her father trampled across the flowers in the hall, his boots tearing apart lilies and roses. Shay set everything on the counter and followed him toward the bedroom.

"Why the hell would you do something like this?" he yelled, the sound sudden and loud in the house. Shay fell against the wall in the hallway.

She heard Dana. "Maybe if you weren't so sorry, this wouldn't have happened."

"You can go," her father said. "You don't live here no more, remember?"

"Well, it's done anyway. No reason to be mad about it now." Dana came down the hall, belly rising and falling, grabbed a pot of lilies, and slammed the door behind her. Shay heard her car start up in the yard and pull out of the driveway. It was just the three of them now.

Her mother was trying to explain, voice too low for Shay to hear. Shay stared at the leaves, petals, and stems ground together in the hall, chewed under her father's feet. She listened so hard that she could hear a high ringing all around her, her shoulders stiff and legs sweaty from the swing.

"You're gonna carry them all back. Every damn one."

Shay could hear them coming, so she ran out of the hallway and into the living room and then out the door, moving farther and farther away from them, not wanting to see her parents' faces. She stood in the yard until her mother came through the door carrying an armload of flowers, the wreath around her neck. Her mother walked straight down the road toward the cemetery, the flowers held to her chest, and she did not cry.

Shay went back inside and found her father shaving in the bathroom, listening to the radio like everything was fine. She went to her room, took the sheaf of flowers off her pillow, and put them in her backpack. She zipped it up and slid it under her bed.

Shay sat at the table while her father stood over the stove, making a pan of tomato gravy and some fried biscuits, the sound of hot grease searing flour and the scrape of the fork against the bottom of the pan. They ate together while her mother came and went like a ghost.

Her father finally showered and went to bed. Shay found her mother sitting on the edge of the couch, holding a phone book in her lap and running her fingers over its cover. She tugged at her mother's sleeve. "I have to show you something," Shay said.

Her mother shook her head.

"It's in my room," Shay said. "You can have it."

Shay gave up and went to get it herself. She pulled the backpack out from underneath her bed, looked at the door to make sure her father wasn't standing there watching, and opened the bag. Inside, her roses were the color of ash.

When Shay touched them, they disintegrated, big flakes like burned newspapers rushing out of the bag in a cloud, filling the small space and moving into the hallway. The cloud was dark and hot, and it was all Shay could see. It charred the walls and floors, coating them in black, sweeping through the house. Finally, it lifted to become a greasy stain on the ceiling tile, and the air cleared.

On the walls, there were shapes in the soot, stems and leaves and blossoms. Images of flowers were charred into every surface, across the whole house. Shay ran into the living room and found her mother, looking around at the walls and floor. Her mother began to laugh hard, her voice cracking and eyes watering she laughed so much.

"He'll burn the damn house down," she said, and kept laughing. "He'd do anything to keep me from having something."

Shay got a brush from underneath the sink and scoured the walls, but she couldn't get them clean. She scrubbed and scrubbed, her knuckle busting against the plastic handle of the brush, blood running down her hand. Down the hall, her father slept in a room where flowers were burned into the walls, waiting for him to open his eyes and see. And over her shoulder, her mother held onto the phone book and laughed, waiting for morning.

BLUEBEARD'S DAUGHTER

after "Bluebeard," by Charles Perrault

Part 1—Bluebeard's Youth

The supermarket has green tile floors. Bands of fluorescent light ripple over it, Blue's boots unlaced and heavy. Blue's beard is long and black, braided thick like his hair. He wears an old denim coat, gone ratty at the cuffs, and carries a produce sack of cherry tomatoes to the checkout counter.

He sees the scars on the cashier's wrists. Short brown hair. Mousy girl, pale with big, hollow eyes. The ragged scars.

"You're coming home with me," he tells her.

She laughs. "You think so?"

"It pretty much has to happen."

She grins. "Well don't look so sad about it, blue eyes. Five ten for the tomatoes."

He gives her a five and picks up his sack. "I'll be waiting outside."

"You're a funny guy. I don't get off for a while. If you're still waiting, I guess you could buy me dinner."

Two and a half hours later, the cashier walks outside, white apron slung over her shoulder. Blue is leaning against his car, a convertible painted up like the Red Baron with black Maltese crosses on the doors.

"Shit," she says. "What do you do for a living?"

He motions for her to get in. "Restore old cars. My name's Blue."

"Samantha. You know, I've heard about you. One of the cart guys, Tim, he tells stories."

Blue shifts and pulls out of the parking lot, the wind fluttering the stray hairs hanging over his forehead. "Mexican okay? Stories. What kind of stories?"

His voice is rough and he is a big man and older than her and she is a little afraid, and she loves it. "He says you fuck girls, and then you kill them."

Blue sighs. "Sounds like Tim's a cock-blocking piece of shit, and I need to talk to him."

She laughs again, her body tense, roller coaster excited. She thinks, anything can happen with a man like this.

At the restaurant, they get a booth, Samantha sliding across the red vinyl to be next to him, Blue putting his arm around her. They order dinner, then split some ice cream, sit there together for a while.

"Want me to tell you how I got this?" she asks him, holding up her wrist. "People always ask."

He eclipses the scar in his big hands and shakes his head. "I know."

A few months pass. Mostly it's good. Samantha has moved in with him, rattling the locked drawer of the desk in the den, but he won't give her the key. He comes home from the shop one day and can tell by the distinct kind of quiet in the house that she has broken in.

Blue finds her in the den, staring at a stack of photos fanned across the desk. "They've all got the same look," Samantha says.

Blue touches the photos. "They all killed themselves. This is all I have left."

Trying not to sob, Samantha says, "I guess I know what you saw in me."

He holds her and strokes her cheeks with his wide palms. "Let me tell you about them."

A dancer, the two of them students together, by gunshot to the head. A brunette teacher broken down on the roadside who he'd stopped to help, by hanging. A clerk, a police secretary, a vet. Pills, pills, poison. A willowy bank-teller by cutting. A hitchhiker by pills, the same day he'd picked her up.

"I'm surprised you can keep going," she tells him.

He is crying now, big man, all of him, holding her with his face in her chest and sobbing.

Before he leaves for work the next day, he covers everything with post-it notes. *Don't kill yourself today!* On her toothbrush. The refrigerator, the computer, closet doors, the silverware drawer, everything she will touch that morning. He empties the medicine cabinet before he leaves, threw out all their kitchen knives a long time ago.

He comes home and she's gone. Finds her dead under a pine tree behind the house. She'd climbed all the way to the top so that she could jump. His heart moves fast and he grabs handfuls of his own hair and pulls at himself. This hurt is familiar, losing everything.

Part 2—Bluebeard's Prime

Married, Blue's wife is pregnant. A daughter. They will call her Violet.

He has stopped going to work the last month. He tells her that he can't trust her to be alone.

His wife stands in her underwear in the kitchen, her body tiny like a frog's, belly-skin stretched balloon-tight. She tries to smile. "You could leave me a note reminding me not to kill myself."

"Don't ever say that again."

There is nothing to cook in the house, but she won't go with him to the store, and he won't leave her by herself. He finds half a tomato in the refrigerator, cuts it into quarters, eats it. He sits down beside her on the couch, her stomach between them.

"Surprised I made it this far. You know?" she asks.

He goes away for a moment and comes back with a yellow notepad and a pencil. "I'll make you a list of all the good things in the world."

She stares at Blue without blinking while he lists and lists and lists. Sparrows' nests, irises, cicada shells. Lake water, blue jeans, tube-tops. Sunshades, chrome, the seven thousand red species of tomato. That night, she kills herself after he finally falls asleep. When Blue finds her the next morning, he swears never to love again.

Part 3—Bluebeard's Age

Blue's boots are too heavy for his feet now, but he wears the same jean coat, gone black from oil stains. His desk has been locked for years. He can't remember what he did with the key. He has retired from the shop, sees no one, goes nowhere. It bothers him.

Blue goes to the adoption agency and files papers. The agent is tall, her hair silver blond. She laughs like music. "Can I buy you lunch?" she asks him.

Blue shakes his head. "You're lovely, but not my type. You look like someone who could live forever."

She laughs, not understanding. "How can I help you?"

"An older kid," he tells the agent. "Someone who can mostly take care of themselves. Someone to talk to."

The agent tells him there are three kids: Marcus, fifteen; Samuel, eleven; and Violet, seventeen.

Blue groans. Had she been born, his daughter would be nearly this age.

"About the girl." The agent pulls out a file. "She's had some problems." The agent starts to tell Blue things, but he closes the file in his big, veined hands. "I know," he says. "I know, I know, I know."

Months of paperwork, and finally Violet is getting into his car, her hair brown and short. Her skin pale like porcelain. "I like your car," she says.

The Red Baron has aged better than he has. Every day, someone calls him wanting to buy it.

"I guess they told you about me," she says. "Hurting myself."

Blue laughs. What else can he do? "Girl, there is nothing you've done to yourself that I haven't seen."

They find a routine. Her going to the courthouse in the morning to take a class, finishing her GED. Him working in his garden, scouring the house of anything she might use to kill herself. Them watching movies and not knowing how to talk to one another in the evenings.

One day, she is scraping filth out from the back of the kitchen cupboards, when she sees something metal caught between the boards. She shoves her hands back into the tight space to get it, catching a splinter in her thumb. She pulls the key out, gray and dirty, beads of blood pulsing out of her finger and running over the metal. It takes her only an hour to find the desk drawer.

Blue comes in from gardening, recognizes an old quiet. He washes his hands in the sink, but does not hurry. He finds her in the den, a stack of photographs on her lap.

"Who are all these women?"

"My whole, bad life," he says. He tells her everything, woman after woman, suicide after suicide. She tells him about trying to kill herself in her foster home, being taken to special doctors. They talk for the first time.

"I see why you picked me," she says.

"You're not going to be like them," Blue tells her.

"I thought I had a chance. I thought things were getting better." She sets the photos on the floor. "But now I know I'm not going to make it."

Blue takes her by the shoulders and pulls her out of the room. "Come here. We'll make a list."

They sit down on the couch, and Blue hands her a notepad and a pen.

"I don't blame you. I want you to know that," she says.

He kisses her on the forehead.

"What am I going to list?" she asks.

"All the good things in the world. Whatever you think is good. But you have to do it yourself."

The girl stares at the paper for a long time. When Blue thinks that he's lost her, she writes something. "You have a badass car. And you said I could drive it when I get a license."

He nods and puts his arm around her, staring at her pen.

She writes something else. "Garden tomatoes. And the tomato worm we found."

She keeps writing. He buries his face in her shoulder, feeling her arm moving. She is writing and writing. His hope is such a small thing.

BONES

OLDJOHN'S HOUSE

WAY OUT IN ARIZONA, a few miles from the desert reservations, Oldjohn and his five kids lived. His kids were all in their thirties, and Oldjohn hated them. They were failures, even Fatjohn who'd only ever wanted to work at the gas station down the road, and they'd lived with him their whole lives. They stole his whiskey, ate all his pension could buy, and ran off every woman he'd had for the last fifteen years, starting with their mother. But they were too big for Oldjohn to whip anymore, so one day he decided to build a house that could whip them for him, and whip them good.

He built the house on the edge of his land next to the highway. It took him four months to collect enough scraps from woodpiles and abandoned houses, but Oldjohn was a good hater—the only thing he was good at—and kept at it until he had enough lumber and tin. The day Oldjohn went to build it, he brought with him heaps of old belts, coat-hangers, cut-off lengths of water hose, tough branches, and everything else good for whipping children. All these Oldjohn hung inside the walls and put up in the attic as he built the house. Each still throbbed with the hurt of his children and with his own disappointment, and he packed them in so thick that nothing could be inside the house without feeling their sting.

For weeks he worked. Finally Oldjohn finished, clapped the dust off his hands, and went home. His kids were in the living room smashed together on the couch in front of the TV: Fatjohn, I'mjohn, Meanjohn, Miranda, and Candace. The couch was broken down almost to the floor underneath them. Miller beer bottles rolled around their feet, and yellow popcorn flakes were ground into the rug. They were watching a western. On the screen, Indians chased buffalo across the plains in Toyotas, the small trucks heaving up and down over potholes and hills, feathers whipping from the side mirrors. Miranda and I'mjohn were ignoring the movie and playing cards. Oldjohn saw their dark hair and skin, their tall bodies, and remembered their mother. He stepped in front of the TV.

"I've built you all your own house by the highway," Oldjohn said. "Now get the hell out." His kids cheered and shouted, all talking at once and running back to their rooms. They filled laundry baskets and army duffel bags with everything they had, which wasn't very much. I'mjohn took the cards he and Miranda played with all the time. Miranda took the family size bottles of shampoo and conditioner she needed for her long, thick hair. Meanjohn and Fatjohn helped each other carry the TV. Candace, last to leave, went to the pantry and measured out some dry beans, rice, and noodles into grocery sacks. She kissed Oldjohn on the cheek on her way out. As their voices receded down the hill, Oldjohn locked the door so that they couldn't come back.

He sat down alone and started drinking, rushing to the window when he thought he heard one of them outside, but there was never anyone there. The house was quiet, and for the first time in years he could hear the wind sobbing through the cracks around the windows and pushing through the crawlspace under his feet. He took one last hot swallow of whiskey and lay down on the couch. He stayed there for a long time, not knowing what else to do.

The sun was hot and white, and Oldjohn's children went squinting down the side of the hill to their new house beside the road. When they got to it, they huddled together in its ragged, ugly shadow. The house was tall and narrow with two floors. Its sides were mismatched planks of sand-scarred wood and irregular pieces of tin, flecked with rust and peeling back at the corners. I'mjohn stepped onto the porch and took the doorknob in his hand. The others crowded around him. They swung the door open and looked inside. The house was as dry and dusty as a shipping crate. Besides the porch, there were two big rooms one on top of the other, a small kitchen, a bathroom, and an attic. There was no furniture at all inside. They decided I'mjohn and Meanjohn would live upstairs and Miranda and Candace would live downstairs. They made Fatjohn stay in the attic. The five of them played cards the rest of the evening, grinning to each other because they now had their own house and wouldn't have to fight with Oldjohn all the time. Then, after they became tired, they spread their blankets out on the floor and went to sleep.

In their room, Miranda and Candace stayed up talking like they always did. Finally, Candace grew tired and started to say her prayers. Miranda kept interrupting her and changing the words: "Dear Lord, bless me," Candace would say. "With a big man to warm my bed," Miranda would finish. "Let us have the strength to withstand," Candace would say. "His lovely body on top of ours," Miranda would finish. They went on like this until Candace was too frustrated to pray, and Miranda was already dreaming of men.

That night, Candace couldn't get any rest. The house was so empty, she was sure that she could hear everyone's breath echoing off the walls. Every gasp, snort, and snore floated down the stairs and ricocheted around the room until it struck her in the ear and made her bolt up in the dark. It went on like that for hours, until she couldn't stand it anymore. Candace ran out of the house to find something to fill all that emptiness. While the others slept, she kept filling.

In the morning, no one could say anything for a while. There was a national park service picnic table in the living room. Road signs were tacked to the walls—their directions all confused—a charcoal grill was in the kitchen, a dismantled eighties model Ford truck was hung in pieces along the wall going up the staircase, sacks of gardening dirt were stacked in the corner, oranges were scattered over the floor, and Miranda found a duck in the closet. I'mjohn even found a bicycle chained to the faucets in the bathtub and had to sit on it while he showered.

"It's like Christmas," Fatjohn said. They heard someone pull up in the yard and went to the window to look. Candace parked a white Buick on the lawn next to three others. She got out, opened an umbrella to shade herself from the sun, and started walking back toward town to steal another.

The four of them made a breakfast of the oranges and sat down at the picnic table to discuss what they should do. Fatjohn and Meanjohn insisted that there was nothing that could be done. She was their sister, after all, and wasn't the house better now? I'mjohn could tell that Miranda was bothered by it, though. He followed her into the kitchen and helped her clean the grill to cook lunch. They whispered together as they scraped charred tinfoil off the grillwork and raked out the old coals.

"She'll go to jail," Miranda said, "and all of us will go with her."

I'mjohn nodded. "I don't care if she is our sister. We have to do something before this comes back on us."

They decided what they would do. I'mjohn walked up the hill to Oldjohn's house. He didn't try the door, but opened his old window and stepped through. I'mjohn called the police department and told them that his sister had been stealing cars and where she'd put them. As he hung up the phone, Oldjohn walked out of the bathroom. "You're back," Oldjohn said.

"No, I only needed to use the phone."

Oldjohn nodded. He brought I'mjohn into the kitchen and made him a cup of coffee. I'mjohn thanked him for the coffee and told him about how much they were liking their new house.

"It's bad," Oldjohn said. "It's not a good house, and you should get out."

"No, it's great. We like it."

"There's nothing good here, and you should leave."

I'mjohn finished his coffee and thanked his father again. He told him not to worry. He went back to the house with the TV remote, a cook-pot, and a new bottle of whiskey. The police had already taken away Candace and the cars by the time I'mjohn got back. He and Miranda made lunch. Afterward, they sat at the table raising shots to their sister for most of the night and tricked the duck into drinking with them.

The second morning, they all had a bastard of a headache, and everyone was quiet. Fatjohn locked the front door twice, but each time he went back, it was unlocked again. He looked up at the house's ill-joined walls and ceilings looming over him and locked the door a third time. He walked away for a minute, but when he came back, it was open. The brass mouth of the lock, scratched all around from the teeth of keys, looked as surprised as he did.

Fatjohn went to Miranda first and shouted at her, "Why do you keep unlocking the door?" She covered her ears and told him to be quiet, that she hadn't touched a door all morning. Then he went to his brothers and shouted at them, "Who keeps unlocking the door?" They yelled and threw their shoes at him, told him to get the hell out. But it only got worse. All morning, Fatjohn went along locking doors behind him and finding them unlocked as soon as he turned his back. He could hear them click open as he stepped away. By lunchtime, he was beating the doors with his fists and screaming that something was wrong with the house.

Meanjohn's head felt full of waves and he couldn't stand Fatjohn's noise anymore. He found his brother swearing and trying to take the front lock apart with a screwdriver. Meanjohn pounded on his brother's head and back with both fists and chased him up the stairs and into his room. Then Meanjohn stopped, his eyes lifting to the ceiling. Since they'd moved in, none of them except for Fatjohn had been inside the attic. Hanging from the ceiling were hundreds of old belts, pieces of water hose, stretched out coat-hangers, and branches. They drifted back and forth from the wind blowing in through the window and rattled softly together. For a moment, Meanjohn was very afraid, remembering all the whippings Oldjohn had given him as a child. But then he laughed. "This house is just as screwed up as anything he ever did." Fatjohn nodded, hoping his brother wasn't angry anymore, but when Meanjohn jerked down some of the belts, he knew that he was in trouble.

Meanjohn bound his brother's feet and hands, rolled him onto his stomach, and striped his back and legs with welts while Fatjohn screamed for him to stop. Finally Meanjohn left the room, noticing that the doorknob had been put on backwards. He locked the door from the outside, giving it a shake. "What do you think about the locks now?" He walked back to his room. The floor creaked under Meanjohn, and it kept sounding like someone was coming up behind him. But each time he looked over his shoulder, no one was there. He would feel better after he lay down, he thought.

Later, I'mjohn opened the bathroom door and saw Miranda stepping out of the shower. Both hands were up wringing out her hair, and one leg was over the edge of the tub, long thigh tapering to calf and foot, a halo of water around her toes. The water made her hair gleam black and her skin wet and bright like honey. I'mjohn saw her and was still for a moment. Their eyes met, and he shut the door slowly and walked back to his room.

They always locked the door when they were in the bathroom, and neither knew how something like this could have happened. They didn't cook together that night, but stayed at opposite ends of the house. Meanjohn went back and forth asking them what was wrong, but they only got angry with him and wouldn't say.

Finally, the two of them met again at Fatjohn's door. He was beating on it from the inside, yelling for someone to let him out. I'mjohn shrugged. "I can't get it to open." Miranda tried, but she couldn't open it either. They started laughing about it, just chuckling at first, then more and more as Fatjohn yelled at them from the other side of the doorway. They leaned against each other and laughed until they were crying. "I'm sorry," said I'mjohn when he could finally speak. Miranda shrugged. "It was an accident. We don't have to talk about it." They decided to go play cards while they tried to think of some way to get Fatjohn out of his room.

Knowing that they had forgotten him, Fatjohn made a rope from the belts and tried to climb down through the window. Halfway down, the belts came undone all at once, and he hit the ground hard. The belts rained down on his face and chest. He threw them off and went to the front door, ready to yell at his brothers and sister for leaving him there. He tried the doorknob, but it was locked. He shook it, knocked on it, kicked it, but nothing did any good. No one heard him and came to open the door. "Fuck all of you!" he yelled. He walked back up the long hill to his father's house. He went to Oldjohn's door—one he'd been going in and out of all his life—and tried to open it. He broke down into sobs. Oldjohn's door was locked too.

He walked away, babbling to himself and kicking at the cracked dirt. "All the doors in the world are shut to me!" he said. He liked how it sounded and said it again, crying. This had always been true, he thought, it had just taken him this long to see it. He walked out to the highway beside the gas station where he had never been able to get a job and hitched a ride away from Oldjohn, his cruel family, and this cruel place.

In the house, they'd finally gotten Fatjohn's door open with a pry bar, but he wasn't there. They decided he must have gone back to Oldjohn's house, and it was getting late anyway, so they didn't think any more about it. After dinner and a few hours of TV, they started getting ready for bed. Meanjohn had been acting strange all day, but I'mjohn didn't care to ask him about it. I'mjohn put the duck in the bathtub for the night, hoping it would be easier to clean up after in the morning, and went to bed. But every time I'mjohn had almost fallen asleep, Meanjohn would roll over on the other side of the room and hit the floor with his fist.

After the fifth time, I'mjohn sat up. "What is wrong with you?" he asked.

"The house is creaking. The boards around me keep making noise."

"All houses creak. Especially Oldjohn's houses."

"No," Meanjohn said. I'mjohn could dimly see him sitting up on the other side of the room. "This sounds like someone is walking toward me. Like someone is sneaking over here to get me while I'm sleeping."

"No one is in here but you and me."

"I'm telling you, I can hear them!" His brother sounded hoarse and afraid.

I'mjohn was too tired to have patience for this. "That must be an awful thing. Still, if you don't stop hitting the floor so I can sleep, I'm going to beat the hell out of you."

"I have to do something to keep them away!" said Meanjohn.

I'mjohn got up, grabbed his boot, and walked over to his brother. Meanjohn hit the floor when he heard someone walking toward him, then yelled when he realized someone was really there. I'mjohn beat his brother good with the boot, his fist buried inside it and punching Meanjohn in the stomach and chest, until he was tired and went back to lie down. Not even ten minutes had passed, and Meanjohn started yelling and throwing things again. I'mjohn threw both boots at him, called him a shithead, and took his blankets downstairs.

He walked down the staircase to Miranda and Candace's room, knowing there would be space because his sister was still in jail. In the soft blue light coming in through the window, he could see Miranda sitting on the floor with her arms wrapped around her knees. He wasn't sure if she could see him. Then he heard her talking.

Miranda was missing her sister and remembering their prayer. "Dear Lord," she called out. "Bless me with a big man to warm my bed. Let me have the strength to withstand his lovely body on top of mine."

At once, all I'mjohn could remember was his sister's honey-colored skin stepping out of the shower. She saw him then, standing on the other side of the room, but didn't recognize him in the dim light. She knew only that he was tall and lovely and watching her. She rose, and they met each other in the middle of the room where the light from the window couldn't reach. It was a long time before Miranda recognized I'mjohn, and by then it was too late.

Meanjohn found them in bed together the next morning. They covered themselves and were afraid of what he would say.

"You left me all alone up there!" Meanjohn shouted. "I fought them all night by myself!"

Miranda held the blankets to her chest and looked worried. I'mjohn said that he was sorry.

"There's something wrong with this house," Meanjohn said. "And I'm going to do something about it." He went outside.

I'mjohn and Miranda started putting their clothes back on. With every garment, they looked stranger and stranger to each other, and they didn't like it. Outside, they could hear Meanjohn ripping into the side of the house.

"I liked it," said I'mjohn. "I liked it an awful lot."

"I liked it too," said Miranda, "but we shouldn't have done it."

A section of wall collapsed and the sun fell on them like an eye. Meanjohn stood beside the fallen tin and boards with a black pry bar and a sledge hammer in his hands.

I'mjohn turned back to his sister. "Says who?"

"Says everyone."

"Well, damn everyone. We should do what we want."

They talked it backwards and forwards, moving from room to room. As they talked, Meanjohn was steadily taking the house to pieces. Gaps dotted the walls, letting wind and sand blow through. Meanjohn soon had the second floor and the roof off, and I'mjohn and Miranda couldn't hide from each other.

Miranda walked out onto the porch. She could see the highway and all the cars passing, her father's house above them on a short mesa, and all the other little shacks and houses scattered around. "I love you more than anyone else, but none of them would let us live that way."

"We have this house," I'mjohn said. "If we stay here, none of them have to know about it." Even as he said it, though, Meanjohn pushed down the last wall and started stacking up the boards and tin in the yard. They stood on a porch connected to nothing. Meanjohn was making a big pile of belts, hoses, hangers, and branches, squirting lighter fluid all over it. They went to look.

Meanjohn had found the belts tacked to the insides of the walls and hung up in the attic, under the floors, and wrapped around the rafters. The pile was dense, studded with knots, and taller than any of them. The belts were cracked and split, threaded around dead white branches and sun-bleached water hose, and all the belt buckles shimmered brassily under their patinas of engine grease. "See," said Meanjohn. "This is what was wrong the whole time."

Miranda and I'mjohn looked at each other. They reached for the belts, but Meanjohn had already struck a match and threw it towards the pile. Miranda pulled back I'mjohn's arm as the belts exploded into fire and smoke. "Now, everything will be fine again," Meanjohn said. "Everything will be like it was."

I'mjohn squinted up at the little house on top of the mesa. "This is all Oldjohn's fault."

Miranda started back up the hill. He watched her tall shape shrink as she walked up the hill closer to the sun. He was about to follow her, but Meanjohn handed him a hammer.

"Now we'll put it back right," Meanjohn said.

Miranda went into Oldjohn's house through the window, just like I'mjohn had. She started scooping up coins from tables and dresser-tops. She took his pension check off the mantel, took his wallet and car keys, all the money he had. She'd made it to the hallway when she heard Oldjohn in his bedroom.

He was praying. "Dear Lord, send them away from this awful place. Make them leave," he said. "Everything they ever wanted," Miranda finished.

Oldjohn looked up at her from the bed, but kept going. "There's nothing here worth having," he said. "And Oldjohn still won't let us have it," she finished. Oldjohn began to cry. Miranda threw a handful of coins at him and walked out. She found his old Honda Civic parked beside the porch and took it too.

Miranda saw I'mjohn stop working and watch her drive by, but the pile of belts had burned to ash now, and she knew that there would never be a place for them. She went past him toward the road. I'mjohn scooped up rocks and hurled them at the rear window, shouting that she was just like their mother. Miranda pulled onto the highway and drove off, afraid that it might be true.

The two brothers worked for days putting the house back together. The sunlight was so thick, it stuck to their bodies and made them glow. They looked like angels standing in the desert, slinging up walls of tin and broken boards, their hands and arms throbbing with light. No matter how hard he worked, all I'mjohn could think of was Miranda: the sun desert of her skin, the night desert of her hair. When the house was all back together, they went inside and slept for three days. Then they woke up and showered the light from their bodies, watching it swirl around the drain like fire. They walked around the house. It was just as it had been before, only the belts were gone, and the house lay still and quiet, like something dead. I'mjohn found the duck still in the bathtub and put it on the porch. Meanjohn wanted to go find their brother and sisters and bring them back. I'mjohn told him to go do it himself.

Alone in the house, I'mjohn found his and Miranda's cards and sat in front of the window shuffling and cutting them. He could feel her hands all over them. He could feel her hands all over his skin. He was alone now, without her or anyone else. He looked through the glass at his father's house on the hill, the sun peeling into darker shades behind it. He stayed there for a long time, his thoughts breaking up and reforming like the cards, always the same ideas when they came back together. He wondered if this was how Oldjohn felt.

WATERMELON SEEDS

DOWN ROUND THE OLD LAKE HOUSES, lake people like to eat watermelon. In their tin-bottomed boats sliding over the lake weeds. In dirt yards with dogs slapping tails against legs. On the porches with red juice sticky-dripping over fingers and reddening everything.

Through the kitchen window, Grandpa laughs from the gut. Says, *don't feed them babies no watermelon seeds, or they'll grow vines out their ears.* Little Dino cries and asks, *Is it true, Mama, is it true, Mama?*

Mama listens to the headphone hiss shaking her ears, the slide and pop of bubblegum in her cheek. She snips off watermelon chunks with tick-bird-beak fingernails and drops them into Dino's mouth.

Little Dino gums the melon meat and dribbles seeds down his chin. He cries, *Mama, I swallowed one, Mama, I swallowed one,* and Grandpa shakes his guts with both hands and laughs in the kitchen.

Mama goes to work, and Grandpa puts Dino on his lap. Digs in the boy's ear with fingers black from engine oil. *I feel them vines a coming, little baby,* he says, *I feel them vines a coming.* Dino cries and bites his grandaddy's hairy arm.

That night in bed, Dino dreams of flowers blooming while vines unfurl in his skull and come falling from his head. They push out of his ears, his nose, his mouth. Dino's head is a tangle of watermelon vines.

In the morning, Dino can see nothing, hear nothing, speak nothing. He runs through the house rustling his yellow-flowered head and knocks the TV over, splitting the screen. Mama spanks him so hard that she spits her gum on the floor, then leaves to get a new TV.

Grandpa changes Dino's diaper and finds watermelon juice pooled like blood between his legs. Grandpa takes Dino outside and digs a hole behind the house. He drops the boy inside, mashes him down with a hairy foot until only the vines show. Takes a slow piss on the mound and hums, *grow, little baby Dino, grow.*

That summer, Dino becomes a root, lies like leather in the dirt. His tiny hairs braid into vines that rise and break the gravel round the house. Grandpa's old shack is an island in a lake of watermelon vines, and he laughs and laughs and laughs.

Watermelons come hatching from the patch, their sloped sides like ships' hulls breaking water, and Grandpa gathers them into an old wagon. Sells them for five dollars on the side of the road.

Mama gets heart-sick for little Dino now, forgets about broken TVs, seeds in diapers, and ear-aching Mama-cries. Takes an old shovel and tears apart the patch until she pulls her baby up like a potato. Yanks all the vines and roots off, cleans him pink with the hose. The wind and sun hurt his vegetable skin, and little Dino bawls like a newborn in Mama's arms.

On the roadside, Grandpa makes a killing. New checkered shirts and no more engine grease on his fingers. He breaks a watermelon over his knee to show somebody, a melon-red fetus curled up inside the rind. *Don't swallow them bones,* Grandpa laughs, *I don't know what would happen if you swallowed them bones.*

DESSA AND THE CAN HERMIT

THE WOODS WERE HOT and quiet on both sides of the gravel road. Scattered trash lay in the ditches, its shape bulging up from the orange mud. Dessa carried a stick in one hand and a garbage bag in the other. She wore a green army jacket that hung down to her calves, the sleeves cut back by half. Her black hair fell across her shoulders, swung into her face, and Dessa blew it back. She was hunting cans.

Dessa had been looking for an hour and had found only six cans when she saw a glint of metal under a mound of pine straw in the trees. She pushed through the branches and hit the mound with her stick. A pile of cans fell out of the straw and clattered to the ground. She kicked apart the rest of the mound, a tower of beer cans, easily a sack-full. A sour beer stink rose from the pile. Dessa picked up the first can and was about to put it in her bag when something rattled inside. She shook the something out. It was a dirty finger.

Dessa picked up the finger by the nail, wincing when it flexed, and dropped it into the ditch. She picked up another can and felt something in this one too. Dessa shook out a nose and set it beside the finger. In a few minutes, her sack bulged with the cans. In the ditch, she'd piled all the fingers and toes, clumps of hair and skin, broken rib bones and jelly-red hunks. Together, all the pieces made a shriveled old man with worn-out clothes. He stank like the cans. The man opened his eyes and sat up.

"What are you doing with my home, little girl?" the can hermit asked. "Give me back my cans!"

Dessa waved her stick at him, and the can hermit crawled back from her. "The price of aluminum is up," she said. "Go live in a hole."

She dragged her sack down the road toward her house, cans crashing together inside, while the man followed her on hands and knees.

"That racket!" he said. "This wind! Why did you shake me out of my cans?"

Dessa pointed with her stick to a soda bottle in the ditch. "There's something for you. Take that."

The man jumped on it, stuck his nose inside, and snorted. He threw the bottle at her. "It's not the same."

"Sorry," Dessa said, but kept walking.

The can hermit followed her home. Dessa lived with her mother in a white trailer leveled close to the ground on muddy cinderblocks. It had small windows, and the tin was rusted through in places.

The can hermit stood up and squinted at the trailer.

"You live in a can too," he said. "You should understand."

Dessa gave him a hard look through her hair. "You're an asshole," she told him. She set the bag down beside the concrete steps and wiped her nose with a camouflaged sleeve.

"This light, this air!" the man said. "Please. I'll do anything."

Dessa tapped her shoe with the stick and thought for a moment. "You'll have to do everything I say."

The man nodded, clutching his knees, and said that he would.

A few hours later, Dessa and the can hermit went down to the lake, the can hermit carrying four fishing poles over his skinny shoulders, the lines and hooks getting all tangled together. In his other hand, he held a plastic tub of chicken livers.

They sat on the edge of the dock, Dessa showing him how to bait the hooks and set the cork. "You've tangled this one so bad, I'll just have to restring it," she said.

"What are we doing here?" The can hermit cringed from the sky and open lake. Dragonflies wheeled in the air and struck the water, while frog-sound echoed back from the woods.

"Catfish," Dessa said.

"What do catfish have to do with my cans?"

"Everything, if you want me to give them back."

They glared at each other over the tub of livers, Dessa's hair black and messy and falling over her cheeks, the can hermit's every orifice ringed in dirt. Finally, the can hermit took a chunk of liver in his grimy fingers and baited his hook. They tossed out their lines and waited.

Dessa pulled up the first catfish, thick and shovel-headed and spotted with tiny black leeches, and gave it to the can hermit. "I forgot a stringer. You'll have to hold it." The fish spasmed in the man's arms.

The other corks started to tremble, and Dessa couldn't get them all at once. The can hermit held up the fish by its jaw and swallowed it, tail lashing the insides of his mouth and throat as he shoved it down.

Together, they reeled in the other fish. The can hermit ate these, too, leaning over the dock to lap up lake water. "To keep them still," he explained. His belly was swollen, and Dessa watched the silhouettes of fish come and go across his skin.

When they ran out of liver, the can hermit reached into his side and pulled out his own. They tore it into little pieces and baited their hooks with it, catching more fish. When they pulled them in, the can hermit shook the fish by their tails and smacked their heads until they vomited the pieces of his liver onto the dock. "Give back what's mine," he told the fish.

It was almost dark, and together they'd caught eight catfish, three gar, and an old bass. The mosquitoes were thick in the air, so they grabbed their poles and started home.

"This is great," Dessa said, and smiled at him.

The can hermit smiled back at the girl. "It's not a can, but it's nice."

Dessa heard a vehicle pull up outside the trailer. Her mother wasn't supposed to be home for another hour. The can hermit stood on the brown carpet and looked afraid, holding his bellyful of fish.

"The devil comes without thumbs," he said.

"What?"

Before he could answer, someone knocked on the trailer door. The can hermit fell to pieces: digits clattered to the carpet, limbs broke into bits, his teeth and eyes rolled out of his head, and his stomach opened, sloshing lake water and fish across the living room. The can hermit's pieces crawled under the couch, leaving Dessa standing in a puddle of thrashing fish. The knock came again.

Dessa opened the door. It was the can collector with his thin white beard and straw hat. His truck rumbled in the yard behind him, the wooden frame of the bed piled high with sacks of cans. He rested a thumbless hand on the door frame.

"Do y'all have any cans for me today, Dessa?"

His shadow fell over her in the doorway, and Dessa put her hands in her jacket pockets, pulling it tight around her. "Not today," she said.

The can collector pointed to the mess on the floor. "What's all this here?"

"I went fishing."

He scanned the living room over Dessa's head. "Are you sure you don't have any cans?" He grabbed his pocket, swollen with change, and shook it at her.

"Not this time."

"Lying girl." The can collector pushed his way inside, long legs clubbing Dessa out of the way. He picked up a grape soda from the top of the television, half full and having sat out all morning. He drank down what was left of it, long throat jumping, then tossed Dessa a nickel and walked out of the trailer.

"I'll come by tomorrow," he yelled from his truck, backing into the road. Dessa closed the door.

"What was that about?" she asked. But the pieces of the can hermit moved like a line of ants into the dark hallway, heading toward her room. Dessa piled the fish in the sink and started cleaning up the water with towels.

A key scratched across the lock, and Dessa's mother opened the door. Her dark pants and shirt were spotted with food from the restaurant. She set a bag of fast food on the table: a box of chicken, some rolls, plastic containers of coleslaw.

"How'd you make such a mess?" her mother asked her.

Dessa got a piece of chicken and told her mother about her day, the can hermit and fishing, the visit from the can collector.

"You never know what you might find in a can," her mother said. She and Dessa cleaned the fish and put them away in the freezer. Dessa finished drying the floor, while her mother took a shower with the door open, sending steam and the crash of water through the house.

Dessa's mother had work again in the morning, and when it was time for her to go to bed, Dessa leaned over her—hands scrubbed of orange mud, chicken liver, fish scales, and chicken crumbs—and tucked her in, kissing her mother on the forehead.

Back in her room, Dessa found the can hermit sitting on the floor playing with a red-lipped doll.

"Can I have my cans back now?" he asked.

"No," Dessa told him.

The can hermit struck the floor with a withered hand. "Why?"

"You left me to clean up by myself."

The can hermit fell over and wept, a wet and wheezing sound.

"If you do what I say, I might let you have them back tomorrow."

The man sat up and wiped his grimy eyes.

"If you like, you can sleep on my bookshelf tonight. And you can play with my doll as much as you want."

"A bookshelf is nothing like a can," he said. The can hermit held the doll against his neck and stroked its face.

Dessa turned off her light and got into bed. In the dark, she heard the can hermit rattling her dresser drawers. As she drifted off to sleep, she thought of all they might do tomorrow.

It was cool in the house when Dessa rolled over in bed and set her bare feet down on the floor. Her hair covered her face, keeping the sunlight out of her eyes. She went to her dresser to find clothes, pausing when she opened her sock drawer. Inside, the socks were all mixed together, and each one had a small bulge in the toe. Dessa pulled out a lump of cotton. Confused, she shook a wad of cotton and white fabric out of another sock, then another. Finally, she shook out the head of her doll, its lips grinning at her. The can hermit had made her as comfortable as he knew how. Not knowing what else to do, Dessa put the doll pieces back and found empty socks to wear.

She walked through the house yelling for the can hermit, and he assembled himself from all corners: lumps of him tumbled out of the sink where they'd been resting within the dirty dishes, pieces came from underneath the couch, some floated up to the top of the fish tank and crawled over the edge. Dessa nudged him into a pile with her shoe, and the can hermit sat up and opened his eyes.

"My cans?" he asked.

"Not yet." Dessa took him into the bathroom and pointed at the sink. "I lost my mom's ring down the drain a few weeks ago. You have to help me get it back."

The can hermit bent under the sink and unscrewed a U-shaped piece of pipe. He knocked it against the floor, and gobs of wet hair and toothpaste splat onto the tile. The can hermit pulled a ring out of the mess, rinsed it clean in the bathtub, and handed it to Dessa.

"Now I can go back to sleeping in pieces, aluminum walls, dreaming dozens of separate dreams." He squeezed her shoulder. "You live in a nice can, but one isn't enough."

Dessa looked at the ring for a long time. Finally, she slipped it into her pocket and shook her head. "This isn't the right ring."

The can hermit squinted at her and bent down to the mess on the floor. He dug through the hair and muck, but didn't find anything else. He turned back to Dessa, but she was staring at her shoes, hair and jacket sleeves hanging long and limp.

"It must have washed all the way down the drain," she said.

"What does this other ring look like?" the can hermit asked her.

Dessa shrugged. "Gold. With a diamond. Like most rings."

The can hermit snorted. "Fine. But I want my cans back after this. Hold out your hands."

Dessa cupped her palms, and the can hermit's fingers fell into her hands in a pile.

"Go drop these down all the drains," he said. "With plenty of water."

Dessa shoved one twitching finger down each side of the kitchen sink, flushed three down the toilet, washed one down the bath drain, and one down the bathroom sink. She had four fingers left over—his thumbs and index fingers too big to easily go down the drains—and gave these back to the can hermit.

He wrinkled his brow and worked his arms like he was scraping at something. "There's a lot of pipe down here."

Dessa took him into the kitchen and microwaved some leftover chicken for them. They were sitting on the couch watching TV when the can hermit spoke.

"The devil comes without thumbs," he said, already off the couch and running for Dessa's room.

There was a knock.

Dessa opened the door.

"Any cans for me today, Dessa?" the can collector asked.

She began to shake her head, but the can collector pushed his way into the house before she could answer and started picking through the trash in the kitchen. He pulled out three Orange soda cans and held them up to her.

"Oh. I forgot about those," she said. "But that's all."

He reached into his pocket, swaying heavy with change, and set a few coins on the counter. "Are you sure?" he asked.

"I'm sure."

After the can collector left and Dessa heard his truck rumble down the road, she went back to her room to find the can hermit. He sat in the floor with her socks spread around him, pulling out the pieces of the doll, lining them up on the floor, then putting them back into the socks.

"What's so good about your cans anyway?" she asked. "Why can't you just stay here?"

The can hermit picked her up and set her in his lap, wrapping his grimy arms around her. She could smell the old beer in his skin and ragged clothes, the sourness of sweat. He held her so tight against him that all Dessa could see or feel was the embrace of the old man.

"In the cans, it smells like home and it feels like home and it sounds like home," he said.

He held her that way for a while, until eight ringless fingers came crawling into the room like inchworms, black and reeking from the pipes. He reached down and let finger-bones snap back into their knuckles, a sound like joints popping.

Dessa got to her feet and wiped her eyes with a sleeve, the green jacket smelling like leaves and clay and summer against her cheek. "You can have them back," she said, "but only if you stay close so I can come see you."

The can hermit gestured to the window. "Put me where the wind blows over the can mouths, and the sun shines on the metal, and no one could ever hurt me."

"How do I know you won't just leave if I put you somewhere outside?"

The can hermit shoved his hand into his breast and rooted around inside. He pulled out his brown heart, apple-sized, bouncing and warm, and gave it to her.

"I won't go anywhere without that," he said.

Dessa put it in her pocket, the heart throbbing against her leg. She led the can hermit into her mother's room, pulled away the fallen clothes in the bottom of the closet—the heavy winter coats that her mother had worn when she'd lived places with snow, a long time before Dessa and trailers and restaurant work—and uncovered the sack of beer cans. She unknotted the plastic ties and let the mouth of the bag yawn open.

The can hermit jumped and shouted to see them. He nosed inside the bag of cans like a dog, the sack rattling. Dessa watched him force each one of his fingers into a different can, the digits dropping down into them like lizard tails, then crawl over them to stick his arms and nose into cans further back, and keep crawling forward until he'd sifted his entire body down into them. He hadn't even said goodbye.

She took the bag into her room and set it on top of her dresser by the open window, wind ruffling the top of the bag. From inside the cans, she heard the can hermit singing strange songs, happy to be home.

Her mother opened the door and called her to help unload the car. Dessa ran to show her that they'd found the ring. They ate dinner together and watched a movie, her mother carrying Dessa to bed and tucking her in. On the way out, her mother noticed the smelly bag of cans by the window. She stroked Dessa's face. "You work so hard, you have so little," she said.

In the morning, Dessa woke with something cold against her skin. She pulled it out from the tangle of blankets and saw that it was the can hermit's heart, beating slowly. The sack of cans was gone.

On the counter was a note from her mother and two rolls of nickels: the can collector had come by that morning before she'd left for work, and her mother had given him the cans. The note said that the money was Dessa's; she could have whatever she wanted.

Dessa got dressed and ran outside, down the orange gravel road farther than she ever had before, jacket flapping green behind her, all the way out to the can collector's home by the highway. His yard was full of rain-filled soda and beer cans. Black garbage bins filled with crushed cans were lined up by the porch.

Dessa knocked over the bins, sending a spray of silver discs tumbling over the ground. She kicked through the piles, trying to remember what the labels of his cans had looked like, but she couldn't. She thrashed through the yard for almost an hour before the can collector drove up to see her in his yard, throwing cans into the air and crying. As she searched, she held out before her the brown heart, becoming more and more like a stone in her hand.

How the Weaver's Wife Killed the Motorcycle Man

BEHIND A RIPPED SCREEN, Leah the weaver stared out the doorway of her sandy house. Layers of heat peeled off the asphalt and rose up into the sky over the I-40. Her wife was not home from work at the restaurant, and Leah had finished her weaving for the day.

She heard a buzzing sound and watched a motorcycle man come down the highway, his two tires purring over the road. His shirt was white against the orange hills behind him, his hair brown and sunglasses blue. As he passed, he turned his head toward Leah in the doorway in her green and yellow dress. The motorcycle man struck a pothole he did not see, spun off his bike, and skipped across the road like something much lighter than a man. His motorcycle squealed against the asphalt and thudded into the ditch. The man came to rest a little past her driveway.

Leah ran out to the man and pulled him from the road. Her wife, Billie, would not be home until much later, and they only had one car. The man was not awake, but he did breathe. Leah took him into the house. His skin was peeled back in places, patches lumped up like ground meat, and crisscrossed with cuts deep and wide everywhere else. She cleaned the small stones and grit out of the mess of his skin, applied peroxide to the scrapes, and wrapped him in a blanket. It was one she'd woven herself, the individual threads knitted so tightly that they couldn't be seen.

A few hours later, the motorcycle man woke up and saw Leah sitting beside him. "Bring me liquor," he said. "And a mirror." Leah brought them. She checked her watch. It would still be several hours before Billie was home. "Where's my bike?" the man asked.

"It's outside in the yard."

He nodded and held up the mirror. Leah watched him take it and look at his chest, sides, arms, and face. "Why did you get me out of the road?" he asked. "Look at me. No amount of money in the world is going to fix this. Goddamn you. If you'd left me alone, a truck would have killed me in my sleep."

"I'm sorry," Leah said.

He took another drink and stared at her, tracing with his eyes the patterns of her dress. The green and yellow lines wrapped around her hips, unspooled up her sides, and crossed over her breasts.

"I'll let you sleep," she said. "We'll get you to a hospital when Billie gets home." Leah went quietly out the kitchen door and stood outside wondering what to do.

She watched through the kitchen window until the motorcycle man passed out again. Then she came back into the living room. Her loom was the largest thing in the house, its bars and weights empty after this morning. She moved quietly, grabbed the edge of the blanket, and tugged the man across the dusty hardwood floor. When she had him lying against the bottom of the loom, Leah the weaver touched his skin with her cool fingers. Her nails picked around his wounds until she found a ragged thread of skin. She worked this out, careful not to wake him, and pulled and pulled, until she had a coil of it looped around her finger. The skin was heavier than thread, slicker, and beaded with his blood. She unthreaded his skin and spooled it onto the hooks of her loom, worked it over the bars and stretched it tight.

The motorcycle man was purple without his skin and smelled of meat, but he didn't wake up, only moaned. Leah's fingers worked quickly. She picked at the knotted and broken clumps of skin, smoothed them out, and threaded them across. Leah was used to weaving large blankets and rugs. The skin of a man was a small job, and it only took her a little over an hour to make it whole again. She even took away his blemishes: moles on his back, an old scar over his ear, a birthmark shaped like a hand. She pulled the skin off the loom and laid it over his body. After looking at him, she thought it would be best if she started with his feet. Leah sat over him with her needle and stitched quickly and cleanly, tucking the seams deep and out of sight between his fingers, behind his knees, and in the creases of his arms. When she finished, she tucked the last thread of skin under his armpit and stitched it down so that it wouldn't come loose. He started to awaken.

"What are you doing to me?" He sat up.

Leah picked up the mirror and threw it at him. "Look," she said.

The motorcycle man tilted the mirror at his face, down his neck and chest, all the way down to his thighs. His clothes were in a dirty pile beside him. The wood of the loom was dark with moisture, and Leah's hands were black from blood.

"I'm perfect," he said. "Look at my skin. It's beautiful."

Leah nodded, even smiled. "It's the best work I've ever done."

"Christ, it's so soft. Touch it," he said.

Leah shook her head. "I know what it feels like."

"I said, touch it."

Leah reached out slowly and touched his face. The motorcycle man grabbed her hand and pulled her into his lap. He rolled over and pinned her under him. Leah hit him, tried to shove him away, but she couldn't. She screamed, but Billie wouldn't be home for hours.

§

Billie got out of the car in her black slacks and white shirt. Her apron hung low, filled with change and soggy paper coasters. She hadn't made much money, but she had a phone number from a man who wanted to buy a blanket from Leah. He would pay one hundred and fifty dollars. He would pay them as soon as it was done.

The door was double-locked and the chain was on. Billie stood at the doorway and called for Leah to open it. Leah let her in and wrapped her arms around Billie's neck. She let her body hang from Billie's shoulders and, sobbing, told her everything. Billie listened, staring the whole time at the dirty loom and the bloody blanket on the floor.

She stroked Leah's head. "Shh," she said. "Shh. It's going to be okay. I'll fix it," though she wasn't sure anything she could do would fix it. Billie left Leah on the couch and went into their bedroom. She opened her dresser drawer and lifted a stack of magazines. Inside, lying next to empty thread-spools and band-aids, was an old eight-shot .22 revolver. She picked it up, always heavier than she remembered, loaded it, slipped it into her apron, and walked back into the living room.

Leah was pulling the loom apart, throwing the pieces into the yard. Billie pulled her over to the couch and made her sit. She held her for a few minutes, squeezing her shoulders almost to bruises. Billie kissed her forehead. She picked up Leah's wrist and checked her watch. It was almost six o'clock. "I'll be back later," Billie said. "Go lie down."

Billie drove her brown Buick down the highway. There were thin bars of clouds lined up in the sky, and patches of sunlight flickered across the bulge of the gun in her lap. She kept the radio off and drove fast. Seven miles later, she came to the mechanic's shop. When she pulled in, he was reaching up for the garage door. He stood with the edge balanced across his shoulders and watched her step out of the car.

"Sorry, ma'am. We're closed." Grease smudged the corners of his eyes, the wrinkles there making tiny white stars.

"I'm looking for the motorcycle man," Billie said. "He busted up his bike on the 40. Did he come by here?"

"Oh. Him. I asked another customer to give him a ride into Garings. I don't work on bikes, so I sent him to my cousin's shop." He nodded. "I don't work on bikes," he said again.

"Tell me how to get there," Billie said. The man told her. Billie thanked him and bought a two dollar Powerade out of his vending machine. It wasn't cold. She got back into the car and headed toward Garings.

She found the bike shop, all tin and rust on the corner of an intersection in the middle of town. Traffic was thick in four directions. Several men sat on their bikes outside and talked, the engines off. They watched her, a tall slit sliding across their sunglasses on her way to the door. The sun was going down, and the cement lot in front of the bike shop was filled with golden light. Next to the door, a wrecked motorcycle was propped against the building. The side facing her was scraped of all paint and webbed with bright scratches. Sunlight settled there and flared like an ache.

The motorcycle man was inside leaning over the counter and talking with the owner. The man didn't say much back to him, just nodded and shuffled things on his desk, picking papers up and setting them back down. She didn't have to see the torn clothes to know it was him. She could always recognize Leah's work. Billie walked up to him and waited until he noticed her.

"Ryan's Steakhouse?" The man grinned, noticing the logo on her shirt. "They any good?"

"They're shit," said Billie.

He laughed. "That attitude won't bring in the tips."

"You hurt my wife, Leah the weaver."

The motorcycle man stopped smiling. He looked around the shop for help, but no one moved to help him.

"She's taking apart her loom right now," Billie said.

"I'm sorry."

"A man was going to pay us one hundred and fifty dollars for one of her blankets."

The motorcycle man got his wallet, pulled two new hundreds out of it, and handed them to Billie. She put them in her apron.

"I'm sorry," he said again.

Billie nodded. "I believe you." She put her hand in her apron, pulled out the .22, and put it against his forehead. There weren't any lines running across his brow. She shot him. The motorcycle man fell backward onto the floor, his legs and arms thrashing. Billie lowered her arm and fired again. She slowly cocked the gun and fired again. The tin building echoed the shots. The concrete split underneath him, his body stretched across the long cracks. Billie emptied the whole chamber, not realizing it until the ringing in her ears faded and she could hear the dull click of the hammer tapping empty shells.

People started to stream into the building. From cars still running outside at the stoplight came whole families, mothers and fathers and children. The bikers left their bikes and came in with their leather and sunglasses. People came with sacks of groceries from the store across the street. The bike shop mechanics set down their tools and came over too. They all floated around Billie who stood with her gun pointed at the dead motorcycle man on the floor. Voices swept around the room.

"Who is that?" they said.

"That's the weaver's wife," they answered.

"And who is he?"

"That's the motorcycle man who killed the governor's son."

"But we loved the governor's son," said the people.

"We all loved the governor's son," they said back. "That's why she did it. To get him back for killing the governor's son."

"No!" said Billie. "I killed him because he hurt Leah."

"She was the only one brave enough," they said.

Billie put the gun away. She grabbed the people closest to her and shook them. "No. I killed him because he hurt Leah. My wife, Leah the weaver. I don't even know the governor's son."

But the people weren't listening to her. Now that they knew why she did it, they turned and thanked her in one endless voice. They flowed back outside like a river, breaking apart and going into the coffee shops, the gas stations, and the supermarkets to tell everyone how the weaver's wife had killed the motorcycle man.

"You don't understand." Billie said, but they had all left her there alone in the bike shop. "He hurt Leah. She'll never weave anything again." But no one paid her any attention. Billie went back to her car, got in, and started to cry. Now she knew what Leah had known when she tore the loom apart and threw it in the yard. There would be no way to fix this.

Dog Summer

THEY CAME PANTING DOWN the gravel roads that spiraled through the bottoms around the lake, packs of them hungry and gape-mouthed, yellow dogs by the hundreds. They loped along beside trucks, nipping at the tires, scattering back to the woods when someone leaned out the window with a rifle and cracked off shots at them. They climbed into garbage bins, their tails and hind legs wagging in the air, scattered trash and shredded black plastic around the trailers.

The dogs appeared right after Lijah and his brother Travis pushed an old Chevy truck down the gravel road and into their yard. Lijah had bought the truck himself, the first thing that was completely his. As soon as the black tires settled in the grass with Lijah leaning against the hood and grinning, the sound of barking echoed through the trees. The dogs poured into the yard from every direction, ears and tongues and tails flapping, and jumped against Lijah and his truck. He sat with them in the dirt under the truck's shadow, the happiest he could remember. Daddy stared at him through the tiny front window.

That had been weeks ago, and Lijah was still trying to get the truck to run. Through the screen door, Mama yelled for Lijah's little sisters to stay on the porch. "We can't take you to the hospital if you get bit by one of the damn things," she said. Last night, they had heard the dogs moving around under the trailer, their high whines and thick, watery growls.

"I wanna pet one," Donna said, lying on the porch and leaning over the side.

Elaina pointed. "Look at that one with the missing ear."

His four sisters floated back and forth over the sandy boards in their bare feet, long hair and too-big dresses blowing in the wind. They were of the same palette, same muddy blonde hair and pale skin, same faded cloth of their secondhand dresses, edges bleeding into each other as they crowded on the porch.

"What if they bite Lijah?" Kristy yelled back to Mama.

Lijah looked at the dogs circling the Chevy, pissing on the new tires he'd put on that morning and rolling in its shade. "They won't bite me," he said.

Kristy went down the first step, one foot still on the porch. "When you get it fixed, will you take me to a movie?" she asked him.

Lijah put his tools down and walked towards the house. He took out his wallet to see how much more money he needed for a carburetor. "What movie?"

"I ain't decided," she said, pursing her lips and tilting her head back to consider it. "But just me, not Elaina or Donna or Amanda."

Amanda, oldest of the girls at twelve, rolled her eyes and didn't look at her sister. "He's going to take me to school every morning, and y'all can keep riding the bus," she said.

They all started then, yelling at each other about where they would go once Lijah had his truck, how they would go by themselves. Mama and Travis came out, dressed in their cleaning uniforms. They each had a thin cigarette in their mouths, Mama chewing gum and smoking at the same time. "We're gone," she said, and kissed Lijah on the forehead.

The girls tugged at her arms and shirt as she went down the stairs. "Please Mama can't we go play with the dogs for a bit can't we please?"

Travis laughed and got in the car. "I hope they bite your little asses," Mama said. In a few minutes, she and Travis were gone, the blue Civic disappearing around the bend of the road. The dogs watched it go, but stayed where they were.

Amanda looked at her sisters. "Does that mean we can?"

The girls shrugged their shoulders. They didn't know.

They were looking at Lijah now, waiting for him to choose a side. "I gotta go," he said. "Listen to your mama."

He opened the screen door and went inside. Daddy was in his chair, a beer in one hand and the remote in the other. His eyes were closed under his hat. Mostly, he stayed in that chair. Sometimes, he drove to the bar to talk to his friends or got up the energy to fish. They'd stopped asking him about working again years ago.

Lijah stepped around the soft spot in the carpet where the floor had given out. "I'm going to work, Daddy."

The man opened his eyes for a second, took a drink. "Where's your mama?"

"She and Travis are working. They got the car."

His daddy closed his eyes again.

"Them dogs are still out there. What are we gonna do about them?"

A talk show hissed out of the old speakers. Flies rose and fell in the kitchen sink, others thrashing in the flypaper hanging in the kitchen window. His daddy's eyes stayed closed.

"I'm going now," Lijah said.

He went out the door and told his sisters to stay on the porch. "Daddy's sleeping," he said. "Don't wake him up."

"He's always sleeping," Amanda said

Lijah walked across the yard, dogs scattering like quick yellow leaves. They followed him down the road, his shoes kicking through the white gravel. In his pocket, Lijah's hand rested on the edge of his wallet. He only needed a little more. Oak and sweet gum and poison ivy shaded the road the whole way, the dogs crashing through the thick leaves and sniffing, their tails waving like flags.

The gravel road climbed out of the bottoms and ended at the highway. There was a dead dog here at the intersection, yellow like the others. Somebody had run over his head. The dogs paused to look at it. Lijah could see the gas station coming up in the distance. He stayed on the shoulder. Trucks passed and honked at the cloud of dogs trailing Lijah, bumpers shining in the sun. His truck had an old iron bumper that someone had welded together. There wasn't much chrome on the Chevy. He watched the cars go by and thought he might paint the bumpers white, the body dark red. He could see that.

At the gas station, there were bins of watermelons outside. Trucks were pressed around the small building, most of their engines running, people in the back. The dogs spread out through the crowd, wrinkling their noses at the gasoline smell. Lijah's cousin James was wedged into the back of a long-bed Nissan with seven other people, all of them wearing dirty ballcaps. He waved.

"They need any more pickers today?" Lijah asked him.

James shrugged. "Probably."

Lijah walked into the gas station, one of the smaller dogs running in between his legs, and found the three men having coffee at their table by the window: the pea boss, the bean boss, and the okra boss. They were the oldest men he knew, great big sons of bitches with wide hands and shoulders. Their mouths were twisted, always smirking, their eyes buried in deep creases under their brows. They shuffled cigarettes, a little mound of creamers, and sugar packets around the table while they talked, speaking a language of earth and stones, blind worms burrowing, water swelling the ground. They talked of crops, the slow heartbeats eating the earth and rising until dirty hands gathered them up. They cursed and chuckled to each other. Lijah never knew what they were saying. He didn't know anyone who did.

The clerk looked up for a minute, recognizing him and knowing he wasn't going to buy anything, and tilted her big glasses back down to her newspaper. Then she noticed the dog burying its nose in a candy rack and came around the counter, swatting it with her paper and nudging it outside. Lijah waited by the bosses' table until they noticed him and stopped their talk.

"Do you have any work for me?" he asked.

The three men smiled and drank their coffee. This was how they liked things. They spoke. The bean boss and the okra boss shook their heads. The pea boss pointed through the front glass, at the truck with James in the back.

"Thank you." Lijah went out and jumped into the back with his cousin and the rest. He tried to make himself small, but his arms and legs pressed against the others.

"You got in the right truck," James said. "The pea boss is the only one still paying in cash."

"What are the others paying in?"

"Beans and okra. Keep some of what you pick."

"Hell."

"That's what I said. Where's your brother?"

"Travis and Mama are working today. She got him hired at the plant."

He rubbed an eye with his fist. "That pay well?"

"Better than okra."

The pea boss came out, dogs shrinking away from him, and climbed into the cab of the truck. He pulled out onto the highway and took off, Lijah and James pressed back against the tailgate, a trail of dogs chasing after them and slowly disappearing in the distance.

After a while, the pea boss stopped at a barbed wire fence. He got out and pulled up one of the posts so they could drive through. They crossed a pasture and went through another fence into the pea fields. White five-gallon buckets were scattered through the grass. The pea boss waved his hand at the buckets and wheezed deep in his throat.

Lijah shook the dirt out of his bucket and waded into the rows. The purple pods, long and segmented, were dark against the leaves. Ant mounds swelled between the rows. Lijah pressed them flat without noticing, stomped his boots and swatted his legs when he felt them on his jeans and surging for his skin. There wasn't much he could do for it. Grasshoppers kicked off leaves and burst into the air every time a hand reached to tear off a peapod. Yellow ground hornets, big as Lijah's thumb, rose into the sky or sank into the leaves. From the woodline, dogs crept across the pasture and into the fields, dragging their bellies over the cool dirt and sniffing wetly around Lijah's hands. They picked peas on into the evening.

Lijah thought of his truck, remembered the day he and Travis went to get it. They had stared at the rusted body, the broken back glass, the flat tires, standing there a long time and wondering how they would get it home.

Travis knocked on the door and couldn't get anyone, but he'd found a bicycle pump on the front porch. "Get on it, big guy," he'd said. They had taken turns that afternoon pumping up the tires so they could push the truck out of its ruts in the grass and start it rolling down the road. Lijah leaned through the window so he could push and steer at the same time, looking at the trees and houses framed through his windshield. This was his. They had to stop three times on the way home to air the tires back up, Travis telling Lijah that he was an asshole for getting him to do this.

An ant bit Lijah on the hand, and he crushed it with a dirty thumb, its body becoming the same as the dirt. All around him, Lijah could hear pea pods thumping against the sides of buckets. Sweat slid down his face and stung his eyes. He blinked.

His cousin was beside him in the next row. "What are you gonna do when you get that truck fixed?"

"Get out of the bottoms."

James grinned. "I know what you're after. You going to see that girl we met. The one who lives in Bodcaw."

Lijah smiled, remembering her. Overalls stretched tight over her chest. Thin fishhook hanging out of one earlobe, to keep the skin from growing back, she'd said, until she found her other earring. They'd talked until her dad finished pumping gas, when he came and put his arm around her and pulled her away from them. Then it was over, no chance to even ask her name.

"I could go any place," Lijah said. "Remember how Uncle Jeff packed that old car of his and left?" He wiped his face.

James shoved back one of the dogs that was getting in his bucket. "He's my daddy. I ought to remember him. Clean left, didn't he?"

"Can you blame him?" Lijah asked, dropping another handful of peas into his bucket, wishing he hadn't said it as soon as he did.

James gave Lijah a hard look. "I sure can."

Lijah snatched at a pea and missed, tearing off a handful of green leaves. "I could use the truck to get a job over in Bodcaw. Mama said the tire plant's hiring."

"You worry about money too much. Bible says you ain't supposed to do that, that you're supposed to be like them birds and let God provide." James pointed at crows beating their wings and circling each other at the edges of the field. They looked dirty.

"You ain't read no damn Bible," Lijah said. They didn't say anything to each other after that.

When it was dark and they were tripping over the rows and bumping into each other, their hands pushing through the leaves blind, the pea boss whistled for them to come back with what they had. He waved a flashlight over the truck bed they'd been filling all day, dark purple pea pods curled around each other, red and veined under the light.

The pea boss measured the depth of the peas with his hands and arms, gauges he could understand. He crushed a few pods to paste between his fingers and stuck the whole mess in his mouth, chewing it, nodding and pleased.

He pulled out his wallet and started handing bills out to everybody. It was less than it had been last time. Lijah put it away.

On the way back to the gas station, dogs chased the truck for miles, their eyes shining in the tail lights. When the truck came to a stop sign, they held back and panted, growling at each other, and waited for it to start moving again so they could keep chasing. A few more miles, and Lijah beat on the side of the truck for it to stop and jumped out.

"Where you going?" James asked him.

"Tim ordered a carburetor for me at the garage. He said he'd wait for me."

The Nissan was already pulling away, dogs piling around Lijah's legs and letting it go. James looked back at him and asked, "You think it's going to help anything?"

Lijah wasn't sure what he meant. "Yeah," he said.

It took him almost an hour to get to the garage, feet aching from standing in the pea field and from walking. Tim sat on his tailgate and held his lighter to a fresh cigarette. The flame lit his face in the dark, all black hair and dark skin around his eyes. He lifted his head when he heard Lijah's feet on the gravel.

"You better have my money this time, boy. Been waiting since six."

"I got it. Unless you raised the price on me again."

Tim laughed and scratched his head, hair stiff and moving thickly around his probing thumb. "That ain't an unreasonable idea."

They went into the shop, and Tim motioned for Lijah to sit down on one of the benches. He lifted his feet off the concrete and let them hang in the air, his heels still feeling the pressure of the road. The floor had whorls of motor oil on it, shining in the light and snaking off under tables, piles of tires, and tool racks. Tim came back with a white box, *Holley* printed across the sides, and opened it to show Lijah the silvery white metal of the part. Lijah thought how odd this would look against the film of old oil and dirt that coated the rest of the engine. He pulled out his wallet, bulging with small bills, and counted out the money.

"How many peas did you have to pick to get that?" Tim laughed.

Lijah shook his head.

"I'm gonna finish this cigarette, and then I'm gonna give you a ride home. Don't argue with me about it."

Lijah held the box in his lap, felt its corners digging into his arms he held it so tight. The shop door had been left open, and one of the dogs was standing half in the doorway, watching them. Tim threw a piece of bread from a bag on the worktable. The dog backpedaled into the dark, ran forward and snatched up the bread in its narrow mouth, and ran off again.

§

His mama's blue car was in front of the trailer when Tim dropped him off, parked right next to his truck. Lijah thanked Tim and stood in the yard until he was gone. He opened the passenger door of his truck and set the carburetor inside. He spent a few minutes looking at the Chevy before he went in, the light from the utility pole making the whole yard look white and shadowy, like their trailer was lying at the bottom of a lake. The light glinted on the metal reels and hooks of his fishing poles lying in the bed of the truck, shined on the tackle box and leaky blue ice chest beside them. He'd put these in the truck the first day he'd gotten it, so he'd have them when he went somewhere. A dog rubbed its head against his leg in the dark, and Lijah reached down and scratched it good under the neck. It looked up at him with wet eyes, its tail thumping softly against the fender.

Lijah went inside. The house was dark except for the TV flashing. Daddy sat in his chair, a juice carton on the floor beside him, face broad and eyebrows thick and gray under his hat. He blinked at Lijah when he came in and went back to watching. It was a home shopping program. A woman in a white blouse was selling them gold.

"I got the carburetor today," Lijah said. He sat on the couch.

"People buy this stuff," Daddy said. "How do people buy it?"

The woman stood in a bright room, splayed a hand covered in rings.

"Think I'm gonna find another job if I can get the truck running. I'm tired of working for the pea boss, the bean boss, and the okra boss."

"Your sisters will be working for them next summer. Mama's tired of them asking for things."

Lijah went to the fridge and got his dad a beer, a Coke for himself.

"Your mama will kick your ass for taking her drinks."

"This is the only one I've had today."

His dad's army jacket was lying on the floor. The girls must have been playing with it again.

The woman on TV had the whitest teeth, was laughing at something.

"Daddy, what'd you do in the army?"

The woman held up a long bracelet, looking sharp in the white lights.

"Fight," he said.

"How come?"

Next, the woman showed a necklace, held it to her neck and let the camera zoom in.

"Cause they told me to."

There were commercials after that. Then more gold. His daddy had fallen asleep. Lijah found a blanket on the floor and stretched out on the couch. In their room, he could hear the girls talking about something. Even whispering, their voices cut through the thin walls.

He woke up to a soccer game on TV that no one was watching. Mama yelled at the girls from the kitchen, and his daddy was standing at the window, staring at Lijah's truck in the yard. Lijah got up and walked to the stove, a thin square of linoleum separating the kitchen and laundry room from the living room and bedrooms. He put his arms around Mama, looking over her shoulder. She flicked a short knife, lopping potatoes into chunks and frying them in oil. There was a loaf of bread and some bologna on the counter.

"Hey boy," she said, her voice reedy from smoking. "You got that truck working yet?"

"Not yet. Are you or Travis going anywhere? I need to look at the car again to see how all this goes together."

"You got half an hour. We caught another shift."

Lijah walked outside and found his four sisters petting a yellow dog, her stomach swollen and teats swaying as she beat her tail against the porch. The girls had a package of Christmas bows and were sticking them to her sides. The dog had her eyes closed and face tilted up at the sun, enjoying all this.

Travis was watching them. "Y'all are gonna get sick from that thing."

"Her name's Mama Dog," Donna said, still wearing her purple, one-piece pajamas.

A tick dragged its gray abdomen on slow needle legs across the dog's neck. Lijah ripped it off and threw it into the yard. He brushed his hands on his jeans, wiping away the feel of it.

Lijah got the keys from Travis and pulled the car nose to nose with his truck, popped the hood, and hooked up the jumper cables. His battery was old and secondhand, like everything else. He had no idea if it would work. Lijah let the battery charge and looked back and forth between the car's engine and the truck's, checking to see if things matched. He thought he knew how it was supposed to go.

Travis and Mama came out just as Lijah was taking the parts out of the box and digging around under the truck for his wrenches. It was hot already, and the dogs barely moved when his hand bumped them. Mama unhooked the jumper cables from the battery and they said bye, leaving Lijah working on his truck in the yard.

It went on like this for weeks. Mama and Travis went to work every day in the blue car. When they got home, Lijah's daddy came outside. He would walk around the truck while Lijah worked on it, running a hand over the body and staring. Then he drove the Civic to the bar, not getting in until late in the morning. While Lijah scraped his knuckles blue under the hood of his truck, his sisters floated back and forth to the lake, dragging lily pads into the yard and winding them like garlands around the legs of the trailer.

The dogs and Lijah learned together. As he bent over his truck and found leaky hoses and bad sections of wiring, the dogs spread out through the trailers around the bottoms, learning how to jump up and unlatch chicken pens, how to crawl through open windows, how to run from the shine of sunlight on gunmetal.

§

Late in the summer when the leaves were starting to turn, Lijah had been under the hood of his truck all day, making sure the plugs were connected right, the hoses were on, that it had water and oil. The sun moved across the yard and piles of dogs moved with it, keeping to the shade. While he worked, his sisters took a can of corn and their fishing poles down to the lake for a while, Mama Dog following them. They came back wet and muddy, dragging stringers of little fish through the dirt, brim and perch. The dog trotted behind them, licking the scales off the fish. The girls went inside and got Daddy. They sat on the porch petting Mama Dog while Daddy cleaned the fish with a tiny brown pocketknife. He mounded up scales on the porch, then slit the fish bellies open and pulled out the kernels of corn that caught them, laughing at the faces the girls made and flinging the ropey guts to the dogs in the yard.

Over and over, Lijah thought he was finished, jiggled the key, and nothing. Then remembered and adjusted something else. It should run today, he knew. It should have everything.

When the sun was starting to fall out of sight behind the trees and the air was cooler, when his sisters ran in the yard between dogs who only sat and stared at Lijah, he slid into the seat of his truck, shoved the key hard into the ignition, and turned it. It whined. Nothing. He turned it again. Nothing. He pumped the gas with his foot—not too much, Tim had told him not too much—and turned it again, this time the engine exploding into life and sending birds up from the trees all over the yard. The sound echoed down to the lake and rippled the top of the water. It went all through the trees of the bottoms, sending dogs running to the house from every direction, their yellow paws pounding through the mud and leaves. His sisters jumped to their feet. His mama and brother, miles away at work, knew something had happened and looked at each other, smiling and confused. It was a hell of a sound, Lijah thought, loud and hacking and awful, the best sound he'd ever heard.

Lijah saw Daddy watching him from the porch, hands black from cleaning fish. Lijah couldn't tell what he was thinking. The dogs kept pouring into the yard, so thick you couldn't see the ground for them, all yellow skin and ribs and open mouths. They barked over the sound of the engine.

He put the truck into gear and let it rattle backwards into the road. The dogs moved out of the way. Lijah laughed and hit the dash with his hand. The tires turned and pulled at the white gravel, and he was going then, the front end listing side to side, his hands on the loose wheel. A flood of dogs filled his rear-view mirror, covering the road and running behind him all the way to the gas station. He counted his money and put a few dollars of gas in, all he had left.

Inside, the pea boss, the bean boss, and the okra boss were drinking coffee at their table. They looked at Lijah like they didn't recognize him. He stared at the clerk until she came over to see what he needed. He put some bills down on the counter.

"I bought gas," he said.

"Oh." The clerk took the money and looked at it strangely. Lijah waited for something, he wasn't sure what, and went back outside. The dogs had their noses up and were beating their tails back and forth, smiling at Lijah.

The pea boss, the bean boss, and the okra boss came outside. They circled Lijah's truck in their coveralls, big shadows pressing down on it and making it look smaller. They ran their hands through the bed, measuring it in picked vegetables. The pea boss smirked at Lijah and kept muttering to the others.

He pulled out of the gas station, liking the sound of his tires. He drove around the bottoms some before going home, the back of the Chevy filled with dogs, their claws scratching on the metal as they stood and fell, noses stuck into the wind. Lijah didn't remember how they'd gotten in the truck. It was late when he got home, and the car was gone.

Lijah shut his door and locked it for the first time. Inside, his mama and brother were on the couch. He dropped his keys onto the table.

"Daddy at the bar?" Lijah asked.

Mama nodded. "Said he was gonna meet a friend about trying to make some money. Didn't say when he'd be back." She smiled at him. "We saw you got that truck running."

Travis threw a cup at him, and Lijah laughed. "Yeah. It took a while, but I got it."

"How's it run?" Travis asked.

"Shitty."

"You'll get it running better," Mama said. "I know you will."

"If you two are gonna be out here, give me that blanket so I can go lie down in the hallway."

Travis balled up the blanket and handed it to him, along with a pillow from the couch.

Lijah spread out in the hall outside his sisters' door, hearing them talking in the dark. They had compromised, agreeing that Lijah would take all of them to McDonald's. He knew they'd be up, running over him to get outside, in just a few hours. He thought he should take them somewhere tomorrow. Maybe just for a ride around the lake, but something nice for them. He didn't know how much longer he would be here. He could go to Bodcaw after that, maybe stop at the drive-through and ask if anyone knew the girl with the fishhook earring. Or see if the tire plant still needed help. He could go early and they might let him get a shift in that day. Or he might take the highway out of town, the same road Uncle Jeff had taken, hit the interstate and go and go and go. He rolled into his pillow, yellow shapes of dogs running back and forth behind his eyes, and started to drift off. He could do anything.

The next morning when Lijah woke up, the house was quiet. His daddy was back in his chair, a beer in his hand, TV on. On the kitchen table, there were brown grocery sacks. Lijah saw beer, cigarettes, Little Debbie cakes, and sacks of fruit. Where had it all come from? The girls were gone somewhere. Travis and Mama were sitting on the porch, smoking and not saying anything. Lijah walked outside. His truck was gone.

"Somebody borrow my truck?" he asked. He walked into the yard, not waiting for an answer. Dogs sat alert under the trees, watching him with their ears down. In the yard where his truck had been, his tool set, fishing poles, and tackle box had been dumped onto the ground. The tackle box had come open, the old lures and corks looking dull in the sunlight. He walked back to the porch.

"Where's my truck?"

Mama took a long pull on her cigarette and shook her head. "Ask your daddy." She and Travis got up and walked across the yard, following the road down to the lake. Travis looked back once and shook his head. Something had happened. This was them saying they were sorry.

Lijah went back inside, closing the screen door slowly behind him. His daddy took a drink, eyes focused on the TV. Wrestling was on, the volume off. Two men threw each other around the ring, the floor rocking under their boots.

"Where's my truck?" Lijah asked him.

Outside, the dogs were clambering up onto the porch, pressing their noses against the screen and watching them.

Daddy didn't take his eyes off the TV. "Sold it to a friend. Got good money for it." He looked at Lijah and smiled. "In the fridge, we got some beer. Go get yourself one. You did good."

On TV, one of the men hit the other with a chair over and over across the back.

"Get one," his daddy said again. "You did real good."

Lijah walked to the fridge and opened it, more full than he'd ever seen it before. He pulled out a beer and went back into the living room. The can burned his palm it was so cold.

"Why'd you do that?" he asked.

His daddy was quiet, but Lijah waited, letting the pressure of the question keep building in the room. On TV, the wrestler was still down, the referee and announcer crowding around him, the other holding his chair up to the crowd and screaming into a microphone.

Not looking away from the screen, his daddy began to speak. "Let me tell you how to be a father," he said. Outside, the dogs pawed at the screen door. "You have things you wanted to do, and you set them aside to hang tin and roof houses. You pick peas, beans, and okra all summer. You cross oceans and do what you're told." The dogs got the door open and sulked inside out of the sun. They came one after another, filing in and lying on the carpet, their noses turned toward Lijah's daddy, listening. They pressed against Lijah's legs. "You break your back every morning in fields. There is the sound of crickets, water dripping in the kitchen sink, wind blowing under a trailer, and you hate these sounds, but they never stop." The dogs' heads were resting in Lijah's lap now. They covered him to his waist, weighed down the couch beside him, filled the living room and spread out through the house. Daddy kept talking, and Lijah closed his eyes. "You pick up cans, dig out copper, iron, and aluminum at the dump. You wear-out boots, and there are always more. You feed your kids once. You always have to feed them again."

Daddy looked away from the screen and coughed. "Pop that open and have a drink. You did good," his daddy said.

Lijah opened the beer and took a swallow, eyes closed, hands shaking, truck gone and not ever coming back. He felt breathing on his neck and arms. He opened his eyes and looked toward his daddy—to scream at him, to tell him to count the peas he'd picked, to tell him to feel his knuckles still busted from the truck—but all he could see, panting and crying, their eyes wet and jaws trembling, were dogs.

ACKNOWLEDGMENTS

I HAVE A LOT OF PEOPLE TO THANK. My best friend, Brenda Peynado, for everything. My family: my ex-wife Candace Gonzalez, parents Billy and Melissa Hicks, and my brother Trevor Hicks. The three writers and professors of fiction who have been especially important mentors: Shannin Schroeder, Steve Barthelme, and Elizabeth Stuckey-French. The English department at Southern Arkansas University, the Center for Writers at the University of Southern Mississippi, and the Creative Writing program at Florida State University. New American Press and everyone involved in the creation of this book: David Bowen, Raul Clement, Okla Elliott, Liz Green, Ben Percy, and Wil Oakes. All of the editors and magazines who published my work. The writers who were kind enough to write blurbs for me: Ben Loory, Bob Shacochis, and Jeff VanderMeer.

Working on this collection, I had two go-to readers who helped me work out the kinks: Garrett Ashley and Andrew Rhodes. And at risk of forgetting someone, thanks to all my friends who have supported me and my work: Fabian Araiza, Kilby Allen, Leah Bailey, Laura Bandy, Brittany Bentz, CJ Bobo, Jen Brewington, Alicia Burdue, Chuckie Campbell, Sarah Cantley, Krystal Chenault, Beth Couture, Leslie Creed, Marian Crotty, Karlyn Crowley, Jessie Curtis, Grace Davidson, Kate Dockter, Lindsay Marianna Doukopoulos, Jill Fennell, Roxane Gay, Monika Gehlawat, Laura Goldstein, The Gonzalez Tribe, Diana Gordon, Ashlee Hazeltine, Kayla Henderson, Ben Johnson, William C. Johnson, Sara Bland Landaverde, Rebecca Langston, Kate Lechler, Matt Lewis, Lucas Lowery, Tabitha Lowery, Daniel Kasper, Sydney Kilgore, Joshua Manuel, Billy Middleton, Mary Miller, Ashlie Rae Mixon, Tanja Nathanael, Chris Nelson, Naomi Shihab-Nye, Tyler Orsak,

Jillian Phillips, Daniel J. Pinney, Ellis Purdie, Katrina Bobo-Putz, Kent Quaney, Tina Raborn, Misha Rai, Mark Reagan, Kelly Rigney, Sophie Rosenblum, Donika Ross, Ron Salutsky, Bailey Schroeder, Emma Schroeder, Linda Selman, Melissa Bordelon Shields, Kimberly Shirey, Gitanjali Shrestha, Leslie Singleton, Laura Smith, Jesse Snavlin, Andrea Spofford, Kevin Stemmler, Alli Tharpe, Brittni Traynor, Krissie Treadway, Dillon Tripp, Linda Tucker, Ann VanderMeer, Nathan Waddell, Josh Webster, and Elena Yakunina.

Finally, I want to thank the pine woods, vine-swallowed cemeteries, narrow gravel roads, fallen down houses, cold creek beds, barbed-wire fences, and blood red clay of southwest Arkansas.

photograph © Wil Oakes

MICAH DEAN HICKS is an author of magical realism, modern fairy tales, and other kinds of magical stories. His work is published or forthcoming in places like *New Letters*, *Indiana Review*, and *New Orleans Review*. He lives in Tallahassee, Florida.

CPSIA information can be obtained at www.ICGtesting.com
Printed in the USA
LVOW08s2334050315

429435LV00005B/356/P